"You need to leave with me now," Cade said.

"But I can't," Michelle said. "The basketball game just started."

"Sorry. This isn't up for debate." Tory grasped her teen daughter's hand.

Cade stepped forward. "We'll use the back door. Let's go."

The man Tory was prosecuting right now was ruthless. But he wouldn't let his daughter—or Tory—be Mederos's victim.

Seeing the two together was like staring at a younger version of Tory. Both had long, curly blond hair, a thin build and a sprinkle of freckles across their noses.

Cade went through the double doors, inspecting the corridor on both sides. Empty. "Okay, let's hurry."

Tory and Michelle went first, with Cade trailing behind. Now all they had to do was make it to the parking lot.

A few feet from the exit, Michelle halted. "What's going on, Mom?" She looked over her shoulder at Cade. "Who are you?"

"I'm Cade Morgan, Texas Ranger, and you two are in danger here. I'm here to take you to your house."

He wanted to say so much more. But there was no time for that right now.

Margaret Daley, an award-winning author of ninety books (five million sold worldwide), has been married for over forty years and is a firm believer in romance and love. When she isn't traveling, she's writing love stories, often with a suspense thread, and corralling her three cats, who think they rule her household. To find out more about Margaret, visit her website at margaretdaley.com.

Books by Margaret Daley

Love Inspired Suspense

Lone Star Justice

High-Risk Reunion

Alaskan Search and Rescue

The Yuletide Rescue
To Save Her Child
The Protector's Mission
Standoff at Christmas

Capitol K-9 Unit

Security Breach

Guardians, Inc.

Christmas Bodyguard
Protecting Her Own
Hidden in the Everglades
Christmas Stalking
Guarding the Witness
Bodyguard Reunion

Visit the Author Profile page at Harlequin.com for more titles.

HIGH-RISK REUNION

MARGARET DALEY

HARLEQUIN® LOVE INSPIRED® SUSPENSE

Recycling programs
for this product may
not exist in your area.

LOVE INSPIRED BOOKS

ISBN-13: 978-0-373-44771-8

High-Risk Reunion

www.Harlequin.com

Printed in U.S.A.

And we know that all things work together for good
to them that love God, to them who are the called
according to his purpose.
                          —*Romans* 8:28

To all the Texas Rangers
for their dedication and hard work as police officers.

ONE

District Attorney Tory Carson closed her eyes and drew in a deep, composing breath, but as she released it slowly, an image of the dark-haired, tattooed man intruded into her mind. After a long day at court in El Rio, Texas, a town not far from San Antonio, she'd pulled into her garage and sat behind the steering wheel for a few moments, trying to decompress after an intense afternoon selecting members for a jury in the Diego Mederos trial.

As Mederos was escorted from the courtroom, he'd looked right at her, winked and smiled. The memory sent a chill racing through her body. She'd convicted hardened criminals before as the county district attorney, but this one was different. In his black eyes, she'd seen pure evil lurking behind the swagger he presented to the world. Finally, an angry father had come forward to testify against the man who ran a biker gang and murdered the witness's only son.

Her hands ached from gripping the steering wheel so hard. She pried them away and rubbed them together. When she'd become the DA six years ago, she'd promised herself she wouldn't bring home her cases and ruin her time with her daughter, Michelle. She glanced at the clock on the dashboard and quickly gathered her briefcase and purse, then exited her car.

She was later than she thought and hoped as pre-arranged when she was running behind that Michelle had caught a ride with her best friend, Emma, to the junior varsity's basketball game at the high school gym.

At fourteen, Michelle's world revolved around boys and playing basketball. It was times like this that Tory really missed her husband, Derek, who died two years ago. He was the one who'd gotten Michelle interested in basketball. After he'd come home from work, they used to play together most evenings. Her daughter adored her father. His death had been so hard on both of them. But especially Michelle.

Tory unlocked the garage door and hurried into the kitchen. In case Michelle hadn't gotten a ride, Tory shouted, "Michelle, are you here?"

Silence greeted Tory. Relieved she had time to change out of her suit and high heels before going to the game, she scanned the kitchen and saw evidence—a plate and glass by the sink—that her daughter had come home after school as she usually did every day, especially on game night, and had called Emma down the street when Tory wasn't home by the designated time. As a working mom, Tory was thankful for Emma and her mother being able to help her out occasionally.

Tory set her briefcase and handbag on the counter, then walked through the dining room and living room to the entry hall where she gathered the mail Michelle had put on the table near the front door. Heading down the hallway to the bedrooms, Tory flipped through the mail. Nothing important. She looked forward to relaxing and watching Michelle play basketball.

Tory opened the first bill and reviewed the credit-card expenses. The sound of the shower running caused her to pause at the bathroom. Michelle was still here? She'd be late. Her daughter was the one who always kept Tory punctual.

Tory knocked once, then hurried inside.

Came to a dead stop.

Shards of the large mirror over the counter crunched beneath her shoes.

But what caught her full attention was the blood all over the sink and ceramic top. Bile rose into her throat. She put her palm over her mouth and turned away.

"Michelle, what…" Heartbeat racing, Tory yanked the shower curtain back.

Water pounded against the tub and swirled down the drain.

No Michelle.

Tory ran into the hall. Bright red drops trailed on the floor all the way to Michelle's closed bedroom door. Tory charged forward and gripped the handle, then burst inside her daughter's room.

It was chaos. The clothes from Michelle's closet were flung all over the room along with the contents of every drawer in her dresser and desk. Her basketball trophies, photos and books were swept off the bookshelves. Then Tory's gaze fell upon a skull and crossbones painted in red on the wall over her daughter's bed. Fear flashed down her spine.

Get out! screamed through her mind. As she spun around, her heart thumping against her rib cage, her gaze fell on the window, the lower glass pane shattered. Tory raced into the hallway while fumbling for her phone in her jacket pocket. She made a call to Michelle, but it went to voice mail. She really wanted to believe that her daughter was probably fine and on the basketball court, her cell phone left in her locker in the girls' dressing room. She tried Emma's mom's number, but it went to voice mail too. Tory didn't have a good feeling about this.

The image of Mederos with the skull and crossbones symbol tattooed on his arm as he strutted from the courtroom entered her mind again. He was behind this. He had to be.

As she rushed into the kitchen, grabbed her purse and headed for her car, she called the police chief, Paul Drake. When he answered, she slid behind the steering wheel and started her SUV.

"Paul, someone has broken into my house—" she took a gulp of air "—and trashed my daughter's bedroom. The bathroom… There's blood everywhere." She tried to shake the image from her mind. She couldn't.

"Tory, where are you now?"

"I can't get hold of Michelle. There's a skull and crossbones on the wall in her bedroom. That's Mederos's gang symbol," she rambled while she drove as fast as she could.

Tory saw the stop sign too late and slammed on her brakes as a driver at the intersection pulled out to cross. She jerked the steering wheel to avoid the vehicle and sent her Chevy into a spin.

"Where are you?" Paul asked in a firm, no-nonsense voice.

"I…" Tory tried to control her panic. All she could hear was the thunder of her heartbeat in her ears.

"Tory! What happened?"

Pull it together. "I almost had a wreck." She backed up and turned her car in the right direction, her sweaty palms slipping on the steering wheel. "I tried calling Michelle. She didn't answer. I'm going to the high school gym and praying Michelle wasn't at the house when someone came in." *Praying she isn't kidnapped or worse.* She banned that last thought from her mind.

"I'll send some officers to your house. I'll meet you at the gym."

"Hurry." *Mederos has retaliated before against family members of people who have opposed him.*

But she didn't say that out loud. Going after her or her family members wouldn't really help Mederos's case. There was always another prosecutor who could take over. It made more sense that Mederos would put his effort into intimidating the star witness, but then she had the father in hiding and guarded. Few people knew where—except her and the US Marshals.

Would Mederos have her daughter kidnapped to find where the star witness was kept? The image of the skull and crossbones over Michelle's bed mocked that question. Mederos would do whatever he pleased.

Tory sped up, praying to God to keep her daughter protected. She didn't know what she would do if she lost another loved one, especially her daughter.

As Cade Morgan drove toward his family ranch on the outskirts of El Rio, Texas, he realized it was later than he'd thought. He had only fifteen or twenty minutes to grab something to eat, check on his dog to see if she'd given birth yet and then head back to the high school gym for the basketball game. This would be the first time he'd see Michelle playing on the Mustang High School girls' freshman and sophomore team. Seeing his daughter was the reason he'd taken the job in El Rio, covering this part of the state as a Texas Ranger.

He couldn't be part of her life openly, and years ago he'd accepted that, but he still wanted to be involved with her as much as he could be. He needed to talk to Tory, his high school sweetheart, about what that could possibly be. He'd been back home for only three weeks, and in that time he'd been helping the police chief and sheriff to strengthen the case against Mederos that had gone to trial a couple of days ago.

If he was honest with himself, he'd been putting off talking with Tory. When the Texas Ranger position came up, he'd wondered if it had been a sign from God that it was time for him to return home to live after seventeen years.

As he turned onto the highway that led out of town, his cell phone rang. "What's up, Paul?" The police chief in El Rio, a town with a population of twenty thousand and the county seat, had been a good friend when Cade grew up here. It had been nice renewing that friendship.

"I've sent two officers to Tory Carson's house. She just called. Someone broke into her house and trashed her daughter's bedroom. One of the windows was broken. She said blood is everywhere."

Michelle's room! Cade made a quick U-turn and headed back into town. "Where's her daughter?"

"Tory is hoping at the basketball game. She's heading to the high school gym to see."

"I'm already heading that way. It shouldn't take me long."

"I'll meet you at the gym. If you find Michelle be-

fore I get there, call me and I'll go help the police officer secure the crime scene."

When Cade disconnected the call, he pressed his
foot on the gas pedal. *Is my daughter missing?* The
question froze him to his core. Criminals like Mederos would stop at nothing to walk away from his trial
without a conviction.

Ten minutes later he raced into the high school lobby
to find Tory rushing to a set of double doors that led
into the gym, her mouth set in a firm, determined line.
Her gaze locked with his right before she slipped inside.

Cade hurried his pace, entering the gym seconds
behind her. He caught up with her and halted her progress. "Where's Michelle?"

She yanked her arm from his grip. "What are you
doing here?" she asked in a quiet but furious voice.

"Paul called me to help."

Her eyes swept around the gym and scanned the
floor where the game took place. "Just stay out of my
way."

Several people glanced at them. Cade buttoned his
tan suit jacket so his gun or his badge didn't show and
moved up behind her, searching for Michelle over Tory's
shoulder. "I don't see her playing," he whispered, realizing they were already making a scene.

"Or sitting with her team." Tory shoved her way
through the spectators until she broke free of the crowd
around the doors and quickened her steps toward the
team members and coaches on the sidelines.

Then two players on the opposing team parted and
revealed Michelle out of bounds, throwing the ball
into play.

His daughter was safe. Some of his tension flowed out of him.

Tory kept going while his daughter ran toward her team's basket. A Mustang player passed the ball back to Michelle. Cade wanted to watch, but he needed to catch up with Tory while he called Paul and let him know that Michelle was safe.

Tory stopped at the edge of the home team's bench. Sounds of cheers erupted around Cade, and he looked out onto the court. Michelle had scored. It had been years since he'd been in this gym. He'd been looking forward to seeing her play tonight. But the moment he'd been looking forward to was now tainted with a threat to Michelle because of Tory's job.

"I wish they would take a break. Michelle would never forgive me if I ran onto the court and snatched her off it." Tory stood rigid next to Cade, her arms folded over her chest, while following her daughter's every move. Tension poured off her, her teeth digging into her bottom lip.

A minute later, the fans jumped to their feet, yelling, "Go Mustangs." Forgetting for a few seconds why he was here with Tory beside him, Cade added his encouragement. A girl threw the ball to Michelle who had a better position to take the shot, and she tossed the ball into the air.

The swish as it passed through the net set the crowd off again, and Cade cheered, grinning as though he'd made the shot. "That's the way to play."

Tory threw him a piercing look. Cade sobered.

The visiting coach called a time-out.

"Finally." Tory charged toward the head coach as the players came off the court.

Cade followed.

"Coach Bates," Tory called out.

The balding man glanced in her direction, his forehead wrinkled. He took several steps to Tory. "Is there something wrong, Mrs. Carson?"

"I need to take Michelle out of the game," Tory said while Cade scanned the crowd for any threat, many fans watching what was happening between the coach and Tory. "There's been a threat."

"Against the team?"

"No, my daughter. She's in danger." Tory finally pointed to Cade. "This is Ranger Cade Morgan. He's here to escort her from the gym."

Cade spied Michelle marching over to them, her cheeks red, her blue eyes so like his own, darkening with questions. He touched Tory's elbow and nodded toward Michelle a few feet away.

"What's wrong, Mom?"

"You need to leave with me now. I'll explain everything outside."

"But I can't. The game just started. We barely have the lead."

"Sorry. This isn't up for debate." Tory grasped Michelle's hand, then looked at the crowd still bunched around the exit.

Cade stepped forward. "We'll use the back door." Then to the coach, he asked, "Is it still locked from the outside, but we can leave through it?"

The man nodded, still bewildered.

"Let's go." Cade took up the rear while indicating the exit at the far end of the gym where fewer people stood. "Wait at the door."

Cade continued to assess his surroundings. The man

Tory was prosecuting right now was ruthless. But he wouldn't let his daughter—or Tory—be Mederos's victim. Tory paused at the doors leading into the back hallway where the weight room and a smaller gym were located. Michelle stopped and turned to watch the game.

Seeing the two together was like staring at a younger version of Tory, except for Michelle's blue eyes. Both had long, curly blond hair, a thin build and an oval face with a sprinkle of freckles across their pert noses.

"Let me check the hall first." He went through the double doors first, inspecting the corridor on both sides. Empty. "Okay, let's hurry."

Cade trailed right behind Tory and Michelle, frequently glancing behind him. When they reached the rear exit, Cade went out first, checking the area. Now all they had to do was round the building and make it to his SUV in the parking lot.

He gestured in the direction they should go, his grasp on his gun. Tory grabbed Michelle's hand and headed to the left side of the gym.

A few feet from the corner, Michelle halted and tugged her hand free. "What's going on? You're scaring me." She looked over her shoulder at Cade. "Who are you?"

He pulled his jacket open. "I'm Cade Morgan and you two are in danger. I'm here to take you to your house for Chief Drake." He wanted to say so much more. But there was no time for that right now.

Michelle's eyes widened. "Mom, is that true?"

Tory flashed him a penetrating look, meant to stop him from saying anything else. "Yes. We had a break-in at the house."

But Cade would say or do whatever was needed to

keep them safe. He stepped around the pair and peered around the corner. "It's clear. My SUV is on this side of the parking lot. We'll head for it."

The exit door they used opened. Cade ushered the two around to the side of the building before anyone saw them. He peeked at whoever was coming outside. Three teenage boys, dressed in sweats, left the rear of the gym. They didn't appear to be members of the biker gang.

He quickly covered the short distance between himself and Michelle and Tory.

"Why can't we drive home in our car?" Tory asked as she halted at the front side.

"Because it's been sitting out in the parking lot for the whole town to see and have access to."

"So is yours."

"But I'm not the one they're after."

The color drained from Tory's face.

"Who are they?" Michelle plastered herself against the brick building, distress taking over her expression. "Mom?" She glanced between him and Tory.

"I'll tell you later. We need to do what Cade says. He was your dad's best friend in high school. He has our best interest at heart."

"But why would—"

The sound of motorcycles roared through the air, coming nearer as riders entered the school parking lot, all wearing the skull and crossbones emblem on their jackets.

Trapped.

TWO

Cade poked his head around the corner. There were three bikers. The motorcycles went up and down the rows of vehicles. His SUV was fifty feet away. Too far to run to undetected.

Cade withdrew his cell phone and placed a call to the police station. "I need at least one squad car if not two to come to the parking lot at the high school gym. There are three members of Mederos's gang patrolling the cars. Have the officers put their sirens on."

"Are they looking for us?" The pitch of Michelle's voice rose.

He pulled back while Tory tried to comfort Michelle. Her hands trembled, and she balled them.

"Maybe. Hard to tell. I'm being cautious." Cade didn't want to alarm his daughter so much that she shut down, but she needed to know the severity of the situation.

"Mom, is this about the trial you're prosecuting?"

"I think so," Tory answered.

In the distance the sound of sirens blared. "When I say move, run for the black SUV five cars in. I'll be right behind you two." Cade slid his weapon out of his holster and pointed it at the ground.

As the police grew closer, coming in from two different directions, first one biker left the parking lot, then a second one did, followed by the third gang member when one of the patrol cars came barreling down the street toward the gym. That police officer went after the last biker.

"Go. Now." Cade hurried after Tory and Michelle, keeping his gaze trained on his surroundings. Although all three motorcycles had vanished down several side streets, the sense of being watched plagued him each step closer to his SUV. "Get down when you're inside."

He pushed his key fob to open his doors. Michelle scrambled into the backseat with Tory right behind her. He started to climb into his SUV when one of the patrol officers pulled up. He'd met Officer Sims the other day at the station.

Cade walked over to him. "I need you to check out the DA's car for anything suspicious. I noticed one biker stop for half a minute by her red Chevy Malibu two rows over. Call me and let me know if anything was planted." Cade handed him his card with his cell phone number on it, then returned to the driver's side door and climbed inside.

Tory said something to Michelle, but when he sat behind the steering wheel, Tory pressed her lips together and stared out the window. His daughter lowered her chin and twisted her hands together in her lap.

As he drove toward Tory's house, tension pulsed in the silence of the car. He glanced at the backseat several times en route to her place. With her arms crossed over her chest, Tory caught him looking and narrowed her gaze. Her stiff posture spoke volumes of what she was feeling—no doubt all of it directed at him. At one point they had talked about getting married, then September 11 had occurred and everything had changed.

Cade pulled into her driveway. He wished that Tory and he could talk about their past. That wasn't possible right now, but they would have to eventually, because he intended to discover who had invaded her home, which meant they would have to spend time together.

Michelle jumped out of Tory's car and charged toward the porch, her arms stiff at her sides.

Tory scrambled from the passenger's seat. "Wait, Michelle. Don't go inside yet."

Exiting his SUV, Cade strode toward the house as Paul came out onto the porch. Tory spoke to Michelle on the sidewalk then climbed the stairs to talk to the police chief. Cade hurried toward the pair.

Michelle blocked his path. "What's going on with Mom? Why is the police chief here too? How bad is it?"

For a few seconds, Cade didn't know what to say. "You'll need to ask your mother. I haven't been inside yet."

"Cade, would you join us?" Paul glanced at the teenager. "We need to make some plans—alone."

"Then I'll go inside to my room." Michelle stomped up the stairs to the porch.

"No!" Tory said, reaching for her daughter.

The police chief moved in front of Michelle. "In a moment you can go into the house. Give me a few minutes to talk with your mom."

Michelle looked at each of them, then trudged to the porch swing and plopped down on it, crossing her arms and frowning. "I'm not a baby, you know."

"I know, honey. Just give us a minute." Then she whispered to Paul, "You'd better hurry. She isn't the most patient girl, and pulling her out of the game when she was shooting so well isn't sitting well with her."

Paul planted himself in front of the door. "Before you go inside, I need to tell you what Detective Alexander also found on your pillow in your bedroom. It was a photo of you leaving the courthouse in the clothes you have on today. The word *Boom* was written across it in red. What time did your daughter go to the gym?"

"She told me it would have been about thirty minutes before I came home."

Paul frowned. "That means the intruder had only a small window of time to do this. There could have been more than one of them."

"That means he was probably outside watching. He—they could have…" Tory curled her hands.

Despite what happened in the past, Cade wanted to hold her, reassure her, especially when he saw the color drain from her face in the dim light from the porch. He stopped himself before he did that. Instead he clasped her upper arm, the touch familiar to him and yet strange.

"Michelle is looking," she said.

He slid his hand away, not wanting to give his daughter any ideas about their relationship. He was only concerned for Tory in a strictly professional capacity. They might both work in the justice field, but that was all they had between them now.

No, we have Michelle between us.

"What should we do? I have to protect my daughter."

The quavering in her voice reminded Cade of when Tory as a teenager had told him her mother died. That day their relationship had deepened. The year before he'd dealt with his dad passing away. He'd known what she was feeling at the time. "I'll protect you and your daughter at my ranch until we know what's going on for sure. And I think that Michelle needs to know what's possibly happening here. It's too important to keep her in the dark."

"At your ranch! I'm sure Derek's parents would take us in for a few days." Panic laced her whispers. "I know they live in San Antonio but it isn't too far—"

"Can they protect you two?" Cade cut in. "Do you want to put them in danger too if someone is truly after you…or your daughter?"

Tory shook her head. "Doesn't your uncle live at the ranch?"

"Why do you think I wanted to be a Texas Ranger? I grew up thinking I'd follow in Uncle Ben's footsteps. He knows what he's doing. He used to protect the governor."

Paul shifted toward him. "That's a good suggestion, Cade. When she's at the county courthouse, the police and the sheriff's departments can protect her."

"What's taking y'all so long? I'm starving." Michelle rose, one hand on her waist, reminding Cade of Tory when she was upset with him back when they dated. "What's all the whispering about?"

"You need to tell her what's going on. If you don't want to, I can." Cade stressed the last two words.

Tory glared at him. "I'm her mother, and I'll tell her. But I prefer not to do it on the front lawn. I've seen Mrs. Applegate peeking out her window. I'm surprised she hasn't come outside trying to listen to our conversation. What happened here will be all over town soon, and I don't want to add to it."

Paul backed away a few steps. "We still need to figure out what's going on. Most likely it is one or more members of the Mederos gang. I think y'all need to talk in private. Call me when you're settled in, Tory."

"Chicken," Cade said with a chuckle.

Paul grinned. "Yep. Reminds me of when y'all were dating in high school. Two strong, opinionated people clashing." He tipped the brim of his cowboy hat and nodded at Michelle, still at the other end of the porch.

"You two need to pack your clothes. Let's go into the living room to talk, then you should get what you both need to take to the ranch." Cade glanced at Michelle. "She's coming over here."

"Mom, I'm almost an adult. What's going on? Is this connected to the Mederos-gang case?" She set both fists on her waist.

Tory faced Michelle. "Let's talk in the living room." She slid her arm across her daughter's back.

Michelle shrugged away, her eyes large. "You're scaring me."

Tory pushed the front door wide. "Inside first."

Michelle huffed and plodded into the living room, then whirled around, both hands on her waist again. "Why was the police chief here? Why did you take me out of the game?" She fluttered her hand at Cade. "Why is *he* here?"

Cade clamped his jaw tightly together before he said something he would regret. He wished he had the right to step in.

"Someone broke into our house today right after you went to the game. They smashed your window in and trashed your room and…" Tory swallowed hard. "And the bathroom. When I came home, whoever did it must have run before he could do any more damage to the rest of the house."

Michelle's hands slipped from her waist, and her arms dangled at her sides. "He could have hurt you."

"Yes. We'll be staying at Cade's ranch for a few days while the police process the crime scene and I get a top-notch alarm system. So until then he was kind enough to offer us a place to stay."

Michelle threw a narrowed-eye look at him. "Why him? Why can't we stay at Papa and Grandma's house?"

Tory's eyes closed, and she took a deep breath. "Because they live in San Antonio and you have school."

"It's only twenty-five miles away. You could drop me off at school before going to work. Or how about the hotel downtown not far from the courthouse? We could stay there."

When Cade fixed his blue eyes on Tory and cleared his throat, she quickly added, "Also because this could be connected to the Mederos case I'm prosecuting right now. Cade will be there for our protection. This trial shouldn't last too long. This could be just a prank, or the man I'm prosecuting right now may be behind it. I can't take the chance and ignore what happened."

Tears welled into Michelle's eyes. "Someone is after you? Mederos is the head of the biker gang. I've heard stories…" Her voice caught on a sob.

"I don't know what's going on yet, honey, but as a Texas Ranger Cade will be working with the police on finding out what's going on in addition to making sure we're all right."

A tear ran down Michelle's cheek. "I don't want to lose you too."

Cade's heart ripped in two at the thought of his

daughter's anguish and the years he'd missed. Anger he'd shoved down in the dark recesses of his mind surged to the forefront. Tory should have trusted their love. He should have returned home and claimed his daughter despite Tory's marriage and what she and Derek had told everyone in town. Now it was too late.

"Baby, you aren't going to lose me."

"You don't know that." Michelle's voice rose several levels.

"I'm not going to let anything happen to either one of you." The words came out of his mouth before he could stop them.

"Y'all can't say that for sure. Quit treating me like a child. I'll be fifteen soon."

Tory released a long breath. "We'll talk about this later. Give Chief Drake—and Morgan a chance to figure this out."

"Do I have a choice?" Michelle glared at Tory, then him.

"No, but it's for the best. C'mon. Let's pack up and leave." Tory turned toward the hallway but waited for Michelle to follow.

Cade hung back and trailed behind the two down the long hall. Tory hurried in front of her daughter and closed the bathroom door before they passed it. He started to check the damage out, but Michelle's gasp when she looked into her bedroom echoed through the air. The bathroom could wait. He quickened his pace down the corridor.

When he came up behind Michelle, chaos like a tornado had ripped through the room greeted his inspection. This was not a prank, but the actions of someone who had a score to settle. Some of the clothes were ripped apart. And then there was the skull and cross-bones painted in red on the wall. Was that blood? The sight solidified his resolve no matter what, he would find who did this to his daughter's room.

A tall thin man squatting on the floor rose and removed the toothpick from his mouth. He looked past Tory and Michelle to Cade. "I'm Detective Alexander. I'll be processing the room. Trying to lift fingerprints on some of the drawers and anything else I think the intruder touched. So far I haven't gotten too many usable ones."

"Cade Morgan, the new Texas Ranger assigned to this area. Nice to meet you. Can Michelle come in and get some clothes to take with her?"

"So y'all aren't staying here?" the detective asked as he moved to them in the entrance.

"No, not right now." Tory peered around the man to take in the bedroom.

"I'll board up the window when I finish with the crime scene. I still have the bathroom to process and finish this room so I'll be here for a while."

For a second the words *crime scene* hung in the air. Michelle hugged herself and dropped her head, all her anger from before deflated.

"I appreciate that. What have you already gone through?" Tory put her arm around Michelle, and this time her daughter let her.

"That third of the room." The detective gestured toward the far side. "I'm working my way to the door. So long as you don't touch any wood or pieces of furniture, you can get what clothes and items you need. If either of you see anything is missing, let me know."

"Thanks. We will. Michelle, Cade will stay with you

while you gather what you want to take." Tory pointed to a duffel bag. "Use that." She gave her daughter a hug. "We're going to be all right." When Tory pulled back, she quickly left Michelle with him.

But as she hurried away, Cade glimpsed her shiny hazel eyes. His emotions concerning Tory that he'd locked away demanded their release. He couldn't let that happen. Tory had never really known him or she wouldn't have jumped into a marriage with his best friend to give Michelle a father while he was fighting in the war in the Middle East. Appearances had always been important to her, but she should have waited longer, dug deeper into why he hadn't answered her calls and letters. He'd been on an extended secret mission for the Army Rangers and didn't know anything until he'd returned to camp five months later.

Tory didn't investigate why she hadn't heard from him and perhaps that had been for the best in the long run. He'd learned from her not to let his heart get involved. Being detached had helped him on most of his cases, and in this situation he had more of a motive to solve it quickly. Being around Tory stirred memories he wanted to forget.

Tory hurried into her bedroom, grabbed a suitcase in her closet and swung it up onto her bed. That was when her gaze locked on her pillow. Her photo was gone, but she desperately wanted to see it. Try to pinpoint when it was taken, especially if it was a few hours ago.

Keeping her attention trained on the task at hand, she quickly packed clothes for a few days as well as anything else she might also need during that time. Her hands trembled as she snatched her items. When she shut the suitcase, she lifted the bag from the bed and tightened her grip around the handle to still the shaking. She had to be strong for Michelle.

"Are you ready?" Cade asked from the doorway, his gun and badge no longer hidden. His large, imposing body, from his boots to his cowboy hat, eased some of her anxiety.

"Yes, can we stop and get something to eat before going to your ranch?"

"Sure." Cade sidestepped to allow her to leave the room. "Michelle is in the entry hall."

"How was she packing?"

"She didn't say one word even when Detective Alexander took her fingerprint to rule out hers from the ones that he lifted."

"Does he need mine?" Tory asked.

"I told him I would take care of it and give it to him tomorrow. Michelle needs to get out of here." He studied her for a long moment. "You do too."

"I agree. Let's go." This house had been her home ever since she married Derek over fifteen years ago. She'd always thought of it as her safe haven from her work. Now she didn't know if she could live here again.

When Tory turned the corner in the L-shaped hallway, Michelle stood in the entrance into the bathroom as if she were frozen in place. Her duffle bag lay at her feet. "Michelle." She rushed to her daughter and wrapped her arms around her. "You shouldn't have opened the door."

The white cast to Michelle's face and her stare fixed on the counter covered in blood underscored how grave the invasion of her home was. Whoever did this set out to frighten her.

"Mom, who would do this?" Michelle threw her arms around Tory.

Shudder after shudder rippled through her daughter's body. "Honey, I don't know, but the police will find the person. I don't want you worrying about it. You'll be safe."

Cade approached them. "I won't let anything happen to either one of you. Let's get out of here."

Tory began walking Michelle toward the entry hall. "Ranger Morgan has offered to drive us to get something to eat. How about Juicy Burger Hut? You love their hamburgers and fries."

"First, please call me Cade. My uncle and I don't stand on formality at the ranch." He opened the front door and allowed them to leave first. "Do they still have the best fries in town?"

Michelle remained quiet, but Tory said, "According to my daughter they do. I avoid fried food if possible."

As her daughter slid into the black SUV backseat, shutting the car door, Cade caught Tory before she rounded the hood of the Jeep. "Are you all right? This is a lot to take in."

"I'm not concerned about myself. I didn't want Michelle seeing that bathroom. Did Detective Alexander test it to see if it was blood for sure?"

"Yes, it was, but not human blood. That's all he can tell. The lab will narrow it down."

"I was hoping it was all a prank. Seeing the damage again only makes it crystal clear that it isn't."

Tory paused, rounding the hood of the SUV. "We'll never be safe unless we can find the culprits." She finally said what she was trying to deny since she opened

Michelle's door and saw the trashed room. "Look how hard it has been even getting Mederos to trial."

"I promise you I'll find the people responsible for all this."

"That's a promise you might not be able to keep, Cade. We talked about a lot of things when we were young, and they didn't come true."

"That was then. This is now. I'm good at my job." He moved closer and lowered his voice even more. "And that's *my* daughter in harm's way."

Tension vibrated between them. She had a right to be angry. He hadn't ever wanted to be a father. He'd had his chance and didn't even get in touch with her to tell her it didn't make any difference if she was pregnant, that he wasn't going to marry her or be part of his child's life. The only thing she'd heard from him was through Derek, who had contacted him. Cade had sent his congratulations. When her husband told her that, something inside her died that day. She at least thought he would want to be a part of his daughter's life even if he hadn't wanted to marry her. That was when she decided Derek would be Michelle's father in every sense of the word.

She climbed into the passenger side of the front seat. Too much was happening at once. Mederos had sent a terrifying message today. Michelle met Cade for the first time. They were going to his ranch to stay. Even she felt shell-shocked so she could only imagine how her daughter was doing.

Cade started the engine and backed out of the driveway.

"When can we go back home? I still don't understand why I can't stay at my grandparents'."

At a stop sign, Cade fixed his gaze on her daughter through the rearview mirror. "When this is all settled."

The lights from the street lamps lit the interior of Cade's Jeep enough so that Tory could see Michelle's confusion in her knitted forehead and her teeth digging into her bottom lip.

Seeing Cade and Michelle together highlighted their similarities—height, both taller than most, the shape and color of their eyes, a crystalline blue that drew a person in, and a birthmark on their lower back. Thankfully that was where the resemblances ended, especially his black hair and angular jawline. Her daughter took after her with her long curly blond hair.

Tory started to say something, but Cade cut her off. "Y'all are staying at my ranch. I grew up there and know the lay of the land. Not a lot has changed since I was a boy." He drove through the intersection. "I'll be able to protect you both better there."

"Will I be able to go to school?" Michelle asked, her voice quavering.

"We have two days to figure that out. Maybe one of the fingerprints will lead the detective to who's responsible for breaking into our house."

"What am I supposed to do about meeting Emma and Jodie tomorrow afternoon at the church to decorate for the fall festival? I'm running the ring-tossing booth."

"I'm not sure if that's a possibility anymore," Cade said.

"So, I can't go anywhere? I'm going to a strange house, and I have to stay there? What am I gonna do?"

"Honey, I don't know what's going to happen. But whatever we do will be in the best interest of keeping us safe." Being in a house with Cade wasn't what she really wanted either. But maybe it was a good thing they would be on a ranch outside of town. Michelle could be headstrong and could do something to put herself in danger.

Cade pulled into the drive-through lane at Juicy Burger Hut. Within five minutes he left the fast-food restaurant and continued toward his ranch. A thick silence filled the Jeep. As he drove, he kept scanning the vehicles around him. He noted each one that was behind him, making sure he wasn't being followed.

When he left the lights of El Rio behind, a dark two-lane highway stretched out before him, the only light coming from his SUV headlights and the stars. A sliver of the moon hung in the sky. The hairs on his nape tingled. Just ten more minutes and they would be home. All his senses on alert, he riveted his attention on his surroundings.

"We're gonna be stuck out in the middle of nowhere." Michelle broke the silence, her voice a shaky whisper. "What else are you not telling me, Mom?"

"You know everything that I know."

"My ranch is only ten miles out of town." Cade slowed his speed as he took the S curve not far from his place.

Rounding the last part of the turn in the dark, Cade barely spotted the outline of a black truck in the middle of the road. He swerved to avoid the vehicle, his Jeep heading toward the drop-off on the side of the road. As his SUV bounced down the incline, a tree loomed before them. Cade cut the wheel hard to the right to avoid it. One of his front wheels hit something. The Jeep flipped over and began rolling down the hill.

THREE

At the bottom of the hill, the Jeep ended up on its roof. Tory hung upside down, penned to the seat, her safety belt cutting into her. Silence replaced the sounds of the crash for a few seconds.

As she twisted toward the backseat, a moan penetrated the quiet—it was coming from her daughter. "Michelle, are you okay?" She couldn't see into the darkness enough to tell anything.

In the dim light from the dashboard, Cade moved. The sound of a click indicated he'd unhooked his seatbelt. As he broke his fall downward, he said in a tight voice, "Michelle?"

Another groan followed by her daughter saying, "My arm hurts. I think—" a long pause "—ouch. I'm bleeding."

Tory released her strap and braced herself as she collapsed against the roof. "Can you move?"

"Yes, but glass is everywhere."

"Stay put." Cade used his feet to dislodge the remaining driver's side window. "I need to check the area, then I'll get you two out. How bad is the bleeding?"

"All over my fingers." Michelle's pitch rose.

"Keep your hand over the cut if you can, Michelle." Cade shoved one leg out the gaping hole, glancing at Tory. "Get the flashlight out of the glove box. Use it to see what's going on with Michelle."

Tory retrieved it and clicked it on. Light flooded the darkness while Cade wiggled through the opening where the window had been. As he stood, she scrambled between the two bucket seats, inspecting the back area while she crawled toward her daughter. Glass shards glistened in the glow from the flashlight.

Michelle held her hand over her left arm, crimson red oozing between her fingers, reminding Tory of what had been all over her bathroom. The sight nauseated her. She'd always been queasy when she saw blood, but she couldn't give in to that now. She gritted her teeth and removed her sweater, then used it to swipe away the pieces of glass littering the roof around her daughter, so Tory could get to her.

As she wiggled herself between her daughter and the driver's seat, she shone the light on the wound in Michelle's upper arm. "Take your hand away and let me see it how bad it is."

The second her daughter removed her fingers, more blood flowed and dripped onto the roof. The cut was long and probably deep, but Tory couldn't tell for sure. She took her sweater and tied it around Michelle's arm to stop the flow, then she reached up and found the seatbelt release.

In the distance she heard Cade's voice. Probably calling 911. "I'm going to hold you the best I can as I free you and lower you. You okay with that?"

Michelle, her eyes gleaming with unshed tears, nodded. While she helped her daughter, Cade appeared at the side window closest to them. "I've called the sheriff and Paul. Paramedics are on the way too. I think it's safer staying here. They know where to look for us."

He knocked the rest of the glass out of the backseat window, then used his coat to protect them from the shards. He assisted Michelle out of the car before reaching in and giving Tory his hand.

Strong. Capable. Like the man himself. She'd seen the truck in the road only a half a second before Cade swerved the SUV. Her reflexes weren't nearly that quick. She shuddered, thinking about what would have happened if she'd been driving.

In the distance the sound of sirens echoed through the chilly night air. When Tory emerged from the SUV, her legs refused to hold her weight. Shaking, she collapsed next to her daughter on the cold ground, sending up a silent prayer of thanks to God. Somehow she'd managed to escape two threats on her life in one day.

Eight hours later, dawn broke on the eastern horizon as Cade neared the accident site in a rented car. The truck had been moved to the side of the road. There was a group of law enforcement personnel hanging around the vehicle. A couple of deputies managed what traffic there was since the scene was in the middle of an S curve.

He hadn't talked to Paul in a few hours and wanted to know the latest. He pulled behind a patrol car and parked, then glanced at Tory. Her head, cushioned with his jacket, rested against the passenger's window, her eyes closed. When he peeked at Michelle in the backseat, she was lying down. With her cuts and a couple of bruises starting to appear, she looked as though she'd gone into battle, hammering home she and Tory were both in danger.

They were all exhausted after spending a good part of the night at the El Rio Medical Center that served the area. At least they didn't have to go to San Antonio. The injury that had concerned him the most was the slash down Michelle's arm. It required twelve stitches, but she kept it together the whole time. In fact, she had been unusually quiet, her earlier anger before the wreck gone.

Thank you, Lord. It could've been much worse.

Tory rallied when he opened the driver's side door. "Why are we here?"

"I need to talk to Sheriff Dawson and Paul about what they've discovered so far, then I'll drive y'all to the ranch. Uncle Ben has readied the house and will have breakfast for us."

"I'm glad it's Saturday. I don't know how I would've made it to the courthouse."

"We'll talk about all that later. Rest. I won't be long."

She settled against the passenger side door, and her eyes closed immediately. He'd pulled all-nighters before, but he hoped to grab a couple of hours of rest later today. He needed to be at his sharpest if he was going to protect Tory and Michelle.

Cade shook hands with the sheriff. He'd just started working with him and hadn't known him previously, not like Paul who he'd gone to school with. "Have y'all found anything that leads to the person who left the truck on the road?"

"Now that it's daylight, we wanted to search the surrounding area more thoroughly. As you know from last night, we found human blood in the back of the pickup that hadn't been there long. The marks in the truck bed indicated something was dragged from the back still bleeding. We have latent prints in the cab and on the handle of the tailgate as well as fibers. Not sure from what but I sent it to the lab in San Antonio."

"Any test result back yet? Blood type?"

"Not yet, other than it was human. Should hear soon on that. We did find out that the blood in Tory's house was from a pig." The sheriff glanced at where Cade's wrecked Jeep had been. "I know you said last night you didn't see anyone in the truck because you were too busy trying to avoid crashing into it. But when you got out to check around your SUV, did you glance up at the road and see anything?"

"No, it was too dark. The more I think about the moment I first saw the vehicle, I don't believe there was anyone in the cab. Whoever left it was gone or hiding on the side of the road. If I hadn't had my bright lights on, I might not have been able to avoid the black truck. As you saw, it was parked on the road at just the right place to hinder the chance to stop in time. Who owns it?"

"It was reported stolen in San Antonio last night before the accident. Mark Summers owns it, and the police there have checked into his alibi. Part of the time he was with an officer filling out a stolen vehicle report. The rest of the time he was with his family and neighbors discussing the theft and how to beef up security. San Antonio Police will follow up and interview people in the area where the truck was when it was stolen."

After talking with a couple of his officers, Paul joined them. "I'm going to focus on some of the traffic cams and see if I can catch the truck on any of them last night. Maybe we'll be able to get a picture of the driver that way."

"Who else is involved in the trial of Diego Mederos?" Finding blood in the back of the pickup made Cade wonder if more people than just Tory had been targeted yesterday. Even if they knew it was Mederos who was responsible, without evidence he would get away with a crime yet again.

"Judge Parks is presiding over the trial. But he's on a hunting weekend right now and isn't answering his cell phone. Lieutenant Sanders ran the investigation in my department," Paul said. "I contacted him, and he's fine. Deputy Collins helped from the sheriff's office. I haven't been able to reach him yet either. Also, we received help from Ranger Eastman before he retired. But he lives in Arizona. We left a message on his answering machine."

Cade would call the Texas Ranger he replaced and get his thoughts on what was going on. "I'll contact Eastman. He's an old friend of my uncle's." He looked at his rented car. "I know Sanders, but I haven't met your deputy, Sheriff Dawson. I'd like to work with them since they're familiar with the Mederos case."

"Deputy Collins is my second-in-command and just returned from a well-deserved vacation. A good officer. I'll have him gather up his notes and come by to talk to you. How about this afternoon around four?"

"Sounds good. Call me anytime you have a lead. We could have all died last night. I intend to find who's behind this." Cade looked toward the deputies and police officers spreading out from where the truck had been in the middle of the road. They combed the ground and brush, part of them taking the right side of the highway while the other investigated the left. "Are you bringing in a dog to see if he'll pick up a scent leading away from the vehicle?"

The sheriff removed his cowboy hat, ran his fingers through his gray hair, then plopped his Stetson back on his head. "Yep. Billy still has the best bloodhound around these parts. He's on his way."

Cade pointed to the south. "My land starts there. Check that area too." He wouldn't be surprised if something was discovered on his ranch. If he didn't need to protect Tory and Michelle, he'd be out there looking himself. "I'm going to take Tory and her daughter to my house, then I'm going through it to make sure it's secured."

"I can spare a deputy to park outside your house after the search here."

"Good." Cade touched the brim of his cowboy hat then headed back to his rented four-wheel drive.

As he slipped in behind the steering wheel, Tory opened her eyes halfway, then closed them again. He threw a glance at the backseat, and the sight of his daughter sleeping tugged at his heart. Fifteen years ago, his life could have been so different, if he hadn't been on that secret mission. He couldn't change the past, but he could at least affect the future and what was happening here.

Five hours later, Cade hung up after talking with the retired Texas Ranger about the Mederos case. He intended to pay Diego Mederos a visit later today at the jail, then see Lieutenant Sanders at the station instead of his ranch. He didn't want Michelle to overhear too much talk about Mederos.

Although the biker gang leader was the most likely

person behind the attack on Tory and Michelle, he was also going to dig into Tory's past cases. She would be with him when he picked up her files, so they could review them and figure out who to investigate. Her secretary, Rachel Adams, was coming in to box them up.

The sound of footsteps drew his attention. With his hand on his gun at his waist, he rose and went into the hallway to check. Tory stopped halfway down the stairs, her face pale and full of exhaustion. She combed her shoulder-length blond hair behind her ears, then twirled the end of some strands—a nervous habit she used to do when she was upset and not sure what to do. In that moment he wanted to wrap his arms around her and hold her, make her feel safe.

He broke the long silence. "Did you sleep okay?"

"No, I kept dreaming about yesterday. I finally gave up. At least Michelle is still asleep. How about you?"

"A cat nap."

"Where's your uncle?"

"Fixing lunch. He's determined to do his part by making high-energy food to help keep us going."

The corner of her mouth tilted up. "I got that impression when he kept insisting we eat his breakfast."

The hint of a smile reminded him of the Tory he used to know. He hated to bring up the situation, but time was against them. "We need to talk."

"Yes, before Michelle wakes up. This has taken a big toll on her."

He waved his arm toward the living room. "I agree. She's gone through a lot. How about you?" Not only did his daughter have a long gash on her arm but smaller ones on that side of her body. He was feeling sore, so no doubt Tory was too. The seatbelt held them in place, but they had been jerked around as the Jeep rolled as though they were spinning in a clothes dryer.

All emotions left her expression. "I'll be okay as long as Michelle is." She started for the living room.

Cade trailed behind her. He'd learned to read her easily when they were teenagers. She'd confided in him all the time. The woman in front of him was determined to keep everything bottled up inside her. What had happened to her since they'd dated?

She took a seat in a navy blue lounger as he sat opposite her on the tan couch. "When are we going to my office?"

"After lunch. Paul gave your secretary my cell number. She called. She'll be there at one o'clock to help any way she can."

"Rachel is invaluable to me. She knows what's going on in my office as well as I do."

"Good, we could use her input."

She panned the room. "I like the homey feel to this room."

"You can thank Uncle Ben for that. The house may belong to me, but it's really his home." Why were they dancing around the subject they needed to discuss? After another minute of silence, he finally said, "This might be a good time to talk about what happened between us all those years ago." He knew the case needed to be discussed, but their earlier relationship was standing in their way of working as a team.

"No."

The force behind that one word blasted him. "Because Michelle's nearby?"

She nodded, folding her hands together in her lap.

He'd let that go for the present, but they would be

alone on the ride to town and back. "Then we need to talk about who you think would want to do you harm."

"I've been thinking about that all night. At the head of the list is Diego Mederos, but I have made some other criminals mad at me because I was responsible for them going to prison. I've been aggressive in my prosecution. My vision is to make this county a safe haven."

"I wish there was such a place." That was why he'd gone into law enforcement when he'd left the army, but after all he'd seen, he didn't think such a place on earth existed. Thanks to the Lord there was in heaven. That thought had kept him going when he wanted to walk away and let someone else fight the evil in the world.

"I have to try. Did you know what happened to Belinda twelve years ago?"

"Yes." He remembered hearing about it from his uncle. Belinda had been Tory's best friend in high school, and she'd been shot in a bank robbery because she didn't get down fast enough.

"I'd been in that bank ten minutes before that guy went on a shooting spree, killing Belinda. Five people died that day."

"Is that why you became a DA?"

"I was going to law school already, but that was the main reason I changed the type of lawyer I wanted to be."

"Why did you want to become a lawyer?"

"Remember I was on the debate team in high school and college? That's when I started thinking about it."

"Why didn't you write me about that?" On one of his oversea tours, he'd been in the Middle East when she started going to the University of Texas her second year in college.

"Because I wasn't sure. I still had several years to complete before I could go to law school." She shrugged. "A gal can change her mind just like a guy."

Ouch! Cade had wanted a family. They had talked about it growing up. He'd never really had much of one. His mother had died not long after he was born and his father had passed away in a riding accident on the ranch when Cade was fifteen. His uncle became his only family and his guardian.

Cade glanced toward the entry hall, wondering if Michelle was still in the guest bedroom she and Tory shared. "Just so you know, I didn't change my mind."

She twisted her hands together and ignored Cade's statement. "I'll go through the records at my office to make a list of criminals I've put away, starting with the more serious crimes."

Instead of what they really needed to talk about— their past—they danced around the subject, with Tory clearly ignoring they even had a past. "Then we can check to see who's still in prison. Is there anyone else you can think of besides the people you convicted?"

"No. I've lived here most of my life, and I know a lot of the twenty thousand citizens of El Rio."

"Then how about Diego Mederos? I don't remember anyone like him when we were growing up." Twenty years ago the town was much smaller, but as San Antonio had grown so had El Rio.

"He set up shop here seven years ago. I think he's behind most of the serious crimes in this area. The police and the sheriff have tried to get him for years. But he's never gone to trial. Something always happens to the case—a missing witness or evidence corrupted. So far we've been able to keep our main witness alive."

"How?"

"I'm not at liberty to say. In El Rio I'm the only one who knows where the witness is being guarded by the US Marshals."

"You're talking about the father of the teenager killed—Carlos Dietz?"

"Yes. There were a couple of other witnesses besides the father, but he's the only one who will dare testify. He lost his only child. Two years ago, his wife died in a wreck. Guess who was involved in that?"

"Diego Mederos."

"One of his henchman was supposedly driving drunk and got a slap on his wrist. There was some specula-tion it was Mederos who was also drunk. The car was his, and when he's in it, he's always driving. His fall guy served a year in jail and was set free a month be-fore Carlos was murdered in front of his father. Carlos Senior was very vocal about the justice system failing him and his son." She kneaded the muscles at the back of her neck. "I want to change that perception."

Tory was wound so tightly Cade wondered when she would break. The Mederos case was costing her more than a large amount of time. "Then why didn't the henchman come after Carlos?"

"Because most of the complaints were targeted at Mederos."

Not a smart move on the father's part. Cases like Mederos's caused Cade to question the justice system himself. It was made up of people who were flawed, but in the end everyone had to answer to God. That knowledge always gave him some peace. "I'm going to interview him this afternoon while we're in town."

"He's smart and cruel. Mederos won't tell you a thing." Tory bolted to her feet and began pacing.

Cade sensed the presence of someone else nearby. He looked toward the entry hall and tensed.

Michelle stood in the entrance, tears running down her cheeks.

Tory covered the distance between them and tried to hug her daughter. "Honey—"

Michelle pushed away. "Don't. I hate your job. You're in danger because of it."

Cade rose and walked to them. "Worrying doesn't solve anything. It'll only make it worse. When we know what we're really dealing with, you'll be informed. Then we can decide what needs to be done."

Michelle glared at him. "Were you even a friend of my dad's? Or did Mom say that just to shut me up?"

"I certainly had to get your dad and my nephew out of enough trouble when they were growing up." Uncle Ben's gruff voice came from the end of the hall, but as he moved toward them, it softened. "They were inseparable. They went everywhere together. Their curiosity was mighty huge. Once they wanted to know what would happen if you poked a beehive. That was a painful lesson to learn." His six-feet-six-inch presence took up a large part of the hallway. At sixty he was still in good physical condition and was an expert shot.

"You poked a beehive?" his daughter asked Cade as though she couldn't believe he could have been that stupid.

He nodded once. "Guilty as charged, but in our defense, we were only four years old."

"I don't know about y'all, but I've worked up a

mighty big appetite. I hope y'all are hungry. I fixed a lot."

"That's what woke me up. What did you fix? It smells great." Michelle took a step toward Uncle Ben.

"That smell is our dinner. Chili. I slow cook it. My recipe has won several county fair competitions. I hope you'll stick around to have some."

"I gotta."

"Good. I have a basketball hoop on the side of the barn. Cade and your dad used to practice here."

When the two of them disappeared into the kitchen, Tory sagged in relief. "Now you see why we need to be careful about what we say if Michelle is around. She's going through an emotional stage where everything is black or white. No shades of gray. On top of that, she inherited that curiosity Ben was talking about."

Cade leaned close. "I wonder what else she inherited."

Tory's sharp look sliced through him. She pinched her lips together and stalked toward the kitchen.

Before he could follow her, a knock sounded at the door behind him. When he checked out the peephole, the look on Paul's face didn't bode well. Instead of asking the police chief to come inside, Cade stepped out onto the porch. He thought Michelle needed to know what was going on, but not the brutal facts. "Before you say anything, let's go for a walk away from the house."

Thirty yards away, Paul stopped and faced Cade. "We found a dead body on your ranch near the crash."

FOUR

After lunch, Tory left Michelle with Cade's uncle and a deputy and climbed into the rented SUV to head to her office to pick up her files. The second Cade sat behind the steering wheel, she asked, "What's wrong? Have you heard anything from Paul or the sheriff?"

"What makes you think that?"

"Oh, you tried to hide it, and I'm sure you did from Michelle but not me and probably not Ben. You get this hard glint in your eyes as though you're preparing to take on the world. I didn't say anything because Michelle doesn't need to know the sordid details of this case, but I'm sure you've heard something I'm not going to like."

"I keep forgetting you know me well—" he slid his gaze toward her "—and some things haven't changed since we were teenagers. Paul came to the house."

"When?"

"Right after you went to the kitchen." He backed out of the garage and drove toward the highway.

"You should have gotten me. I'd rather hear firsthand any news of what's happening."

He stopped before pulling out onto the road into town

and twisted toward her. "Let me make this clear. I'm the investigator on this case. Not you. I'll keep you informed as soon as I can, but that's only because you are the district attorney."

Anger bubbled to the surface. "No, the only reason you're appeasing me with information is because I may know information that can help you solve the case. Oh, and if I want to be guarded by someone else, that means Michelle will be too." She stopped talking before she said something else and faced forward. She felt the stab of his gaze, but she didn't look at him. Both Michelle's life and hers were on the line. There was no way she wouldn't be actively involved.

He threw the SUV into drive and headed in the direction of El Rio. When they neared the crash site, Tory saw more law enforcement officers in the field on Cade's ranch with crime scene tape around a location.

Now she knew why Paul had come to the house earlier. "Who did they find?"

"Judge Parks in a shadow grave."

All her earlier anger vanished as reality slammed into her. He was presiding over the Mederos trial. "How did he die?"

"Execution-style. After his body is examined at the morgue, Paul thinks the time of death will be narrowed down but right now best guess is that it occurred between five in the afternoon and nine at night."

"I saw him on Friday as he was getting into his car. He was looking forward to his hunting weekend—away from the rat race as he said."

"You may have been one of the last people to see him alive."

A shiver flowed through her. "Are you going to stop?"

"Yes." He parked behind a patrol car. "I can have a deputy guard you."

"No, I've been to crime scenes before. It looks like they're wrapping it up."

"Before we go, I wanted you to know Paul told me that they found that your brake line had been cut on your car, probably when I saw the biker check your car out. Paul had it towed to the police compound to thoroughly go over your Chevy. He'll have your brakes and anything else fixed."

If she had driven her car home with Michelle inside last night, how long would it have been before her brakes failed? "How can we prevent that happening to your car?"

"I'll take care of that. Let's go. We have a lot to do this afternoon."

Her mind numb from everything that had occurred in the past day, Tory traipsed across the pasture to where yellow police tape was strung up. The medical examiner knelt next to a body on the ground. This was the hardest part of her job. In murder cases, she always went to the crime scene. She wanted to make sure she saw firsthand what had occurred. It gave her a better feel for the crime and helped her when she was prosecuting the case. She wanted the jury to remember the victim and that the person needed justice.

Cade joined Paul and Sheriff Dawson a few feet from the body. "I want a copy of all the photos taken as soon as possible. The death of a judge will cause ripples in Austin."

The police chief removed his cowboy hat and raked

his fingers through his thick brown hair. "Good thing you haven't been on the case from the beginning. Everyone involved in the Mederos case has been notified and procedures are in place. I've asked the Texas Ranger office in San Antonio for more manpower."

"Good. We'll need a guard on the new judge who'll be taking over the Mederos trial." Cade glanced between Paul and Tory. "Is the main witness still secured?"

Paul plopped his Stetson on his head. "When the judge was found, I called the US Marshals' office overseeing Dietz's protection. He's fine, and they're aware of what's happening here."

Sheriff Dawson pointed to a deputy nearby. "That's Collins. I'm putting him on desk duty at the station until this is resolved. He could be a target if Mederos's gang is going after people on his case."

"The same with Lieutenant Sanders." Paul hooked his thumbs in his belt. "So if you want to talk to him, you'll need to do it there. In fact, he'll be interviewing Mederos this afternoon."

"What about the officers' families?" Tory wouldn't put anything beneath Mederos.

"Collins doesn't have any in the area." The sheriff motioned to the man to join them.

"Sanders is sending his family away as we speak."

"Shouldn't he be with them?" If she lost Michelle, Tory's life would fall apart. She had to do what she could to make sure Mederos went to prison, but even that wouldn't stop the violence from the members of the gang. She would go after each one until the threat was gone.

"I wanted him to leave with them, but he said he

wants to work with you and Cade to nail Mederos. He assures me they'll be safe where he's sending them. He isn't telling anyone where they're going." Paul nodded at Collins and the sheriff as he passed them to talk to the medical examiner.

"Ranger Morgan, this is Deputy Collins," the sheriff said.

Cade shook the officer's hand. "I'll come see you at the sheriff's office. I understand you've had a number of encounters with the biker gang these past few years. Joe Buckner is Mederos's second-in-command. I've dealt with various gangs in my different assignments, but I want to know everything about this one. The sheriff told me you're the best one to fill me in on the gang."

"Yes, sir. This execution-style murder has Buckner stamped all over it. Although not ever convicted, he has been suspected of one murder recently in an adjacent county and several others when this gang operated out of El Paso. He's as ruthless as Mederos."

"Good to know. Lieutenant Sanders is interviewing Mederos this afternoon. I'll contact you after that." He turned to Tory. "Ready to go? Your secretary is probably wondering where we are."

"I told her to start boxing up my cases if she got there first."

As they hiked back to the rented SUV, Tory glanced over her shoulder as the black body bag was zipped with Judge Parks inside. He was a good man who had been the perfect person to oversee the Mederos trial. He didn't have any family and he was tough on crime. Maybe that was the reason Judge Parks had been murdered.

When she slipped into the passenger seat, she massaged her temples.

Cade rounded the front of the car and settled behind the steering wheel. "Are you okay?"

"I'll be fine when this is over and Michelle is safe." But as she said that, the throbbing evolved into a pounding against her skull.

"We still need to talk about what happened between us fifteen years ago."

"I know." She dug into her purse and pulled out her migraine medicine. After swallowing a pill without the benefit of water, she closed her eyes and hoped the rumbling in her stomach would subside. "But not now."

"One of your migraine headaches?"

"Yes, I still have them from time to time." Intense stress could bring one on. Over the years she had practiced deep breathing and other techniques to keep the tension at a bearable level.

"Then we'll wait, but not too long because I want to be part of Michelle's life."

Her first impulse was to say no. Years ago he'd made his choice and now needed to live by it. At the very least they should hash out what happened all those years ago. She couldn't avoid it since she was stuck with Cade for the foreseeable future. Instead of replying, she stayed quiet with her eyes closed against the bright light. If this weren't so important, she would have asked him to take her back to the ranch. But she needed to be part of this investigation in spite of the hammer striking against her right temple.

At the police station Cade paused at the entrance to Paul's office. He'd pulled the blinds and turned off the light as Tory lay down on the couch across from the police chief's desk. As a teenager, Tory hadn't had many migraines, but when she did, it was best if she was left alone in a quiet, dark room. When they were at the courthouse in her office boxing up her files, he'd wanted to take her back to the ranch after she'd gone to the restroom and thrown up. He knew this was a bad one, but she wanted him to at least be involved in the interview of Mederos. And the quicker that happened, the quicker they could leave and return to the ranch.

"I'll be back soon." Cade put his hand on the door handle.

"Make sure it's recorded," she whispered, her eyes closed.

"Anything you want me to ask him?"

"Ask him what he thinks he'll gain by killing the judge and others associated with the trial."

"You think he's going to answer that?"

"No, but I want to know his reaction since news of Judge Parks's murder won't be out in the press until next of kin is notified."

"Good idea. Rest." Cade quietly closed the door and let the police chief's secretary know where he would be, then made his way to the room where the interviews were being recorded. Paul and Lieutenant Sanders were inside waiting for him.

"How's Tory?" Paul asked when Cade joined them.

"Hurting, and not just because of her migraine."

"When Judge Parks was selected for the Mederos trial, she was elated. She respected him and knew he would do a good job." Paul glanced from him to Sanders. "Y'all ready? Our boy has been sitting impatiently in there—" he nodded his head toward the TV on the desk "—for the past twenty minutes. We discovered he doesn't like to wait, which we've used to our advantage."

"If Tory didn't need to return to the ranch, I'd suggest leaving him for another twenty minutes," Cade said with a grin. "Or longer."

"And you need to talk to Deputy Collins this afternoon too." Paul took the chair in front of the TV to monitor the interview.

"I wish I'd been in on this case from the beginning, then you two wouldn't have to spend so much time getting me up to speed. Ready, Sanders?"

"Yes, I'll let you take the lead. Maybe someone new might be able to get something worthwhile out of Mederos. According to him, he's a businessman who would like to be left alone to run his business."

"Yeah, I'm sure he does," Cade said, thinking about the past twenty-four hours and how close Michelle, Tory and him came to being killed or injured seriously.

Cade let Sanders enter the interview room first, even delaying a few seconds before he followed. He wanted to see if Mederos gave a different reaction to his presence. The tattoo-covered man seated at the table, handcuffed to it, shifted his black gaze to Cade with a slight narrowing of his eyes. Assessing. Calculating, as only a handful of criminals he'd dealt with in the past had done. As his chin went up a notch, Mederos dismissed Cade and swung his attention to Sanders.

Cade had seen other criminals with a cocky attitude become so overconfident that they underestimated his tenacity. He took the chair next to Mederos, crowding the man, while Sanders sat across from the criminal.

"To what do I owe this little chat? As much as I like

getting out of my cell once in a while, you won't get anything from me without my lawyer present." Mederos smirked.

"That's okay. While we're waiting for him, Ranger Morgan and I thought we would have a little chat between us. You can sit back and nap if you want." The detective's voice dripped with his scorn.

Cade lounged in his chair as though he was here to catch up with a friend. "I can't wait until the regular season starts for the San Antonio Spurs at the end of October. I've got tickets for the opening game. That's only weeks away. Do you follow them?"

Sanders chuckled. "I hope all the way to the NBA championship."

While they discussed their favorite players, Mederos yawned wide, revealing the gold fillings in his teeth.

Cade slid a glance at Mederos. "I guess you aren't a basketball fan. Is soccer your game?"

"I prefer shooting at my target range on my property. It's a lot more entertaining." Contempt filled his features as Mederos closed his eyes as if he didn't have anything better to do but take a nap.

Cade ignored the criminal and continued talking about the Spurs' chances of winning.

On cue Sanders's phone rang. He checked who was calling, then stood. "Lab results might have come back on the truck. I've got to take this." He left the interview room as he said into the phone, "Really? This could be our break on the judge's case..." He closed the door on the rest of the conversation.

Leaving Cade alone with Mederos—as they'd planned. The only indication that the head of the biker gang heard was a slight shift on his chair. His eyes remained closed. Too bad the man couldn't fold his arms over his chest to emphasize his lack of interest.

Sanders returned in a minute and took his seat again across from Mederos. "Not the lab results but good news."

"Great. I want to wrap up the case as soon as possible."

Mederos slowly opened his eyes. "If this is supposed to interest me, it doesn't. I'd like to go back to my cell until my lawyer arrives." He sounded bored, but there was something in his expression, a tic in his jaw, that gave him away.

"Sure, we'll fill in your lawyer. We have a lot to talk about. You can go take that nap you seem to need." Cade looked at Mederos as if he were inspecting a cockroach right before he stomped on him.

"Honestly, I don't think we even need him here. Anything he'd have to add would only be a lie." Sanders put his hands on the table and started to rise.

"I'd clap if I could, but my hands are—" Mederos sneered "—tied up at the moment."

Cade threw back his head and laughed. "You are so right, Sanders. How he got to be the head of a ga— business is a mystery to me. Not much upstairs." Cade tapped his temple.

Thunder descended on Mederos's face, and he sat forward. "One day I'll show you how I did it. You have nothing on me. I know what happens in this county— even while in jail." A cocky grin lifted one corner of his mouth higher than the other.

The lieutenant leaned across the table. "Oh, then you already know about Judge Parks's murder. Interesting, since you're isolated in your cell," Sanders said in a mocking tone.

Cade squeezed his hands into fists. The detective wasn't supposed to reveal the identity of the murdered man. Cade scrambled to save things. "But since you know everything that goes on in the county, you already know whose fingerprints we have tying him to the murder."

Mederos relaxed back. "Since I have an airtight alibi, why should I care? Although when I see the guy, I'll congratulate him."

Sanders came up out of his chair and grabbed Mederos's shirt, dragging him toward him. "You're a lowlife."

Cade put his arm up to loosen Sanders's hold. "I'll take it from here, Lieutenant Sanders. Go cool off."

One hand still in a tight grip, Sanders narrowed his eyes on the gang leader. "Fine. It'll be fun watching Mederos's little brother go to prison." Sanders released his hold and shoved the criminal down into his chair. "You can have him, Morgan." The lieutenant stormed from the interview room, nearly bowling over Sam White, Mederos's lawyer, a shark with a reputation to work for whomever could pay his high fee.

"What's going on in here?" White came inside, closing the door after Sanders left. "You are not to question my client without me being present."

"Have a seat. We've been chatting while waiting for you to show up." Cade checked his watch. "Mederos, I'd be worried that your attorney can't get here faster."

"I was talking with Police Chief Drake about the murder of Judge Parks." White took the only other chair in the room, the one Sanders had been sitting in across from the gang leader. "You can't seriously think my client had anything to do with his death."

"Not directly unless he can be in two places at the same time, but definitely a conspirator."

"On what evidence?"

"The latent prints left in the van used to transport Judge Parks's body to the dump site. They were Pedro Mederos's fingerprints." Cade turned his attention to the gang leader whose face reddened. "Your baby brother was sloppy leaving his prints on the truck's tailgate handle. I would have thought you'd taught him better than that."

Jumping to his feet, Mederos exploded with a string of curse words, his cuffed hands balled. "No one taunts me and gets away with it."

"Is that a threat?"

Mederos thrust his face into Cade's, but he didn't step back. His gaze drilled into the killer's. "No one that works for me killed Judge Parks, especially Pedro. I have no reason to kill the judge. One is as good as another."

Cade wasn't going to get into an argument with Mederos. "I didn't expect you to confess to setting this hit up, but we have enough to hold Pedro on the murder."

"I tell you, my bro didn't do it. Someone else killed the judge."

Cade stared into his black eyes. Mederos's gaze made Cade pause. What if he was telling the truth?

Cade sat at his dining room table, staring at one of Tory's files. His eyes burned as though someone had thrown sand into them. He closed them and immediately an image of Tory splashed across the screen in his mind. The second he'd returned to the ranch after the interview with Mederos, Tory had gone to lie down, her face pale, her eyes dull with pain. He'd wanted to help her up the stairs, but she wouldn't let him. He had to content himself with watching her trudge up the steps, clutching the banister as if it was the only thing keeping her upright.

In the past thirty-six hours his life had changed drastically. His daughter was asleep in one of his bedrooms. His first love, Tory, and once he'd thought his only love, was in another room. He hadn't imagined that would happen when he'd taken the position in El Rio. He'd given up on love years ago and instead focused his life on his job. But now he had the toughest task he'd ever faced—keeping Michelle and Tory alive.

And he wasn't going to do that if he couldn't figure out what was going on. After talking with Deputy Collins, he'd wondered if Mederos was telling the truth about the judge. Collins said that Pedro wouldn't do anything like that unless his brother had ordered it. The deputy had actually been surprised that Pedro's prints were on the truck's tailgate handle. Mederos only cared about a few things—money, power and Pedro. Mederos would have sent one of his other men. His younger brother, more like a son to Mederos, was only eighteen. But Cade had seen his share of young boys who were murderers.

Cade swigged the last of his cold coffee, closed one file and opened another. Matthew Thorne. Released two months ago from prison for armed robbery. He had been Tory's first case as the county's district attorney. Cade knew how Tory felt about anyone who robbed a place with a gun. That case must have triggered memories of her best friend dying in a bank heist. He added Thorne's name to the list of ex-convicts to track down.

He leaned back in his chair and peered at his empty mug. If he was going to do any more work tonight, he needed a lot of extra caffeine. He pushed to his feet and walked into the kitchen to make more coffee.

While it perked, he rubbed behind his dog's ears. She was curled in a ball on her bed in the utility room. Bella hadn't given birth to her babies yet but any day. "At least Uncle Ben will be here. I imagine I'll be tied up a lot in the next week." He'd found the mutt next to his car in a small town outside Houston two years ago. Still a puppy, she'd clearly been fending for herself and not doing a good job. Bella's ribs had been showing her lack of hunting skills. He couldn't *not* take her home with him.

When he returned to the kitchen, he lounged against the counter, trying to clear his mind for a few minutes while the scent of coffee infused the air. The house was quiet—too quiet. He needed to keep moving. After checking the lock on the back door, he made his way through the first floor, inspecting every possible entry into his place. He'd already done this a couple of hours ago and nothing had changed. At the living room window, he paused and peeked outside at the deputy's SUV parked in front of his home. He dropped the blind slat and turned to go refill his mug.

Tory stood rigid in the entrance, barefooted with dark circles under her eyes. "Where's Michelle? I thought we were sharing a bedroom."

"She didn't want to disturb you with your migraine. I put her in another room upstairs."

"Oh, good." She relaxed the tense set of her muscles. "I smelled the coffee. I could use some."

Although not messy, her hair was tousled enough that he didn't think she'd brushed it before coming downstairs. He moved toward her. "How are you feeling?"

"Like I was tied to a Tilt-A-Whirl. But I'm better than I was."

"How's your headache?"

"Down to a dull throb. At least I'm not thinking a jackhammer is trying to split my skull apart. Is everyone else asleep?"

"Yes. Uncle Ben and Michelle went to bed. My uncle will relieve me in a couple of hours." He wanted to run his fingers through her hair. Instead he balled his hands and started for the kitchen. "I could use more coffee. I didn't think the smell would wake anyone up."

"I'm tired, but not sleepy." As she passed the dining room table, she glanced at the pile of files. "Have you gone through all of them?"

"I still have a few more." In the kitchen he took down a mug for Tory, poured the coffee and gave it to her.

She took a slow sip and winced.

"Uncle Ben makes the best. I don't. Add sugar and cream. They help disguise the bitter taste."

After they both doctored their drinks, Cade decided to sit at the dining room table rather than the kitchen one. He needed the files around him to remind him their association was strictly business. They were only together because she and Michelle were in danger.

Yeah, right. Keep telling yourself that.

She drank some more coffee. "You're right. Much better, if you like cream with a coffee flavor. And I do." A small smile graced her full lips.

For a split second, the memory of them kissing before he left for the Middle East inundated him with emotions he'd blocked from his thoughts for years. Love. Wanting. Needs.

"Cade?"

He blinked, not realizing he'd zoned out. "Sorry, just thinking." *About our past.* Now he realized why he'd never come home before to live. She could break his heart all over again, and he just couldn't go through that a second time.

"What names have jumped out for you?"

"I have five names so far that I want to check where they are since they have been released. With most of the big cases, the guys are still in prison, but that doesn't necessarily mean they haven't gotten someone else to come after you. We'll need to look at all possibilities as well as Mederos."

"He's still top on my list. You didn't say much about your interview with him on the ride back to the ranch."

"He denies having anything to do with the murder of Judge Parks, but that's expected. There was an interesting piece of evidence I used against Mederos. It set him off. His young brother's fingerprint was on the black truck."

"The one planted in the middle of the road that we almost hit?" Tory kneaded the sides of her forehead.

"Yep, that one."

"Although Pedro Mederos is connected to the biker gang, he's always been in the background. I've never had any evidence to connect him to a crime in this county."

"So you think Mederos is right? Pedro wasn't involved?"

Tory shrugged. "Anything is possible. Pedro worships his brother. Pedro could have done it if he started worrying about Mederos's chances. Usually the cases don't go to trial."

"Now Mederos has his little brother to worry about. I'll be part of Judge Parks investigation, especially since it is tied to your case."

"I agree there could be a connection."

"I'm especially highlighting the trials you and the judge had in common."

"Did the police find the real crime scene or was the judge killed in the back of the truck?" Tory's eyelids slid closed partway.

"The truck probably was the crime scene. They found the judge's pickup he was using to go hunting. No blood there." When she fought to keep her eyes open, he touched her forearm. "Go back to bed."

"No. We need to talk and this is the best time. No one's up. When Michelle finally goes to bed, she sleeps well. I wish I had that ability."

"Me too." He wanted to cradle her face between his palms and erase the pain and exhaustion he saw there. "I know there isn't a lot of privacy here, and this would be a better time than others, but—"

She raised her arm and laid her fingers over his cheek. "I don't want you—or me for that matter—getting distracted because of our past history. It stands between us and we need to be a team for Michelle now more than anything. Another hour won't make much difference and maybe hashing it out will help us both put our past behind us."

She made sense, but he was afraid to release the pain he held deep inside him. He'd never shared it with anyone, even right after he discovered she'd married Derek, and his baby had been given his best friend's last name.

The feel of Cade's cheek produced good memories Tory had squashed for years. Months had gone by without a word from Cade. He hadn't been captured, hurt or killed. Although Cade and his uncle rarely corresponded, Ben hadn't heard anything from the army concerning his nephew, so he'd reassured Tory that Cade was alive and well.

She'd been at college and turned to Derek for support and help. She hadn't wanted to go home and had even stayed through Thanksgiving at school, but by Christmas and still no word, she'd succumbed to Derek's offer to marry her and give her child two parents. She and Derek had always been good friends, and slowly she'd learned to love him beyond friendship. And he'd been a wonderful father to Michelle.

But she'd always wondered why Cade hadn't contacted her except through Derek.

"Why didn't you contact me about having our baby?" She finally asked the question she'd wondered about many times fifteen years ago.

He stared into space for a moment. "I never got the messages until I returned from a classified mission."

"That lasted almost six months? You never told me you were going to be gone on a secret mission."

"Because I didn't know until five minutes before I left. No one was to know about it—even now. All I can say is that I went behind enemy lines. When I returned, I was debriefed, then given all the letters and phone messages from home that had accumulated. I was reminded the mission was top secret even after the fact. I did tell you of the possibility I would be out of contact for a while before I left for the war zone."

"For that long?"

"I had no control over that. It wasn't supposed to be so long, but the mission ran into some trouble."

"So why didn't you contact me when you returned?"

"I did. Derek answered the phone, and we talked. By that time you were married."

Derek had told her about the call, but she'd thought at the very least Cade would call back and talk personally to her. "I loved you. Why didn't you talk to me?"

Another long pause, then he said, "The truth?"

"Of course, I want the truth."

"I told Derek everything, and I was going to call back. But then he asked me if my appearance all of a sudden would be the best for you. You were due to give birth any day. You were bedridden that last month with high blood pressure. You were married and had a life. One that I had no part of. At that time, I didn't know when I was coming home. *If* I was coming home. I was in a special unit that took risks to keep others safe." A frown carved deep lines into his face. "I wasn't in a good place mentally. Certainly not prepared to marry and be a father."

"You didn't ever call back." And she didn't find out about Cade calling until after Michelle was born. She'd needed to talk to him. Once she'd started to call him but stopped. She wouldn't force herself or Michelle on anyone.

"Derek called to let me know you and Michelle were okay. I asked to talk to you and he said you didn't want to. You were married and had a child to think about."

Her heartbeat sped up, and her breathing increased.

"I never said that. Why didn't you question Derek further?"

"Because I thought he was the best man for you. The war changed me. I was struggling to hold my life together. I wasn't going to be responsible for breaking up your marriage and causing a scandal. You'd made your choice, and I decided to respect that."

"So you walked away from me and your daughter."

"The day before he called me, I'd lost a combat buddy. A sniper took him out. He was beside me one second, the next he went down and I had to scramble for cover. All I could think about was survival." Cade stood and began to pace. "When my time was up, I left the service. I'd given my country four years of my life, but so much more than that. I came back to the States and had to figure out who I was and what I wanted."

The pain in his voice tore at her. She couldn't imagine living in such fear—until now. She rarely had a migraine anymore, and yet the stress had brought one on. The remnants of the headache still plagued her, but thanks to her medication and coping mechanisms she'd manage to nip it before it completely took hold.

"I've only had a little taste of what fear can do and hope to never have it again. Derek should have told me everything, but I can't fault him for trying to protect me. He was a great father to Michelle." She rose and faced him.

"I know. Much better than I would have been right after I returned from the Middle East. I could hear the love he had for you and Michelle in his voice. That's when I decided not to come back to El Rio and find a life somewhere else. That didn't mean I didn't keep up with what was happening. Derek sent me photos of

Michelle. I put them in a picture album. After he died, Uncle Ben did what he could to let me know what was going on with her."

She tried to respond, but the heaviness in her chest threatened to steal her next breath. Tears choked her throat, and she swallowed several times. "I'm glad," she finally said in a hoarse whisper.

"I know it's too late to be Michelle's father, even with Derek gone. In the short time I've been around her, I hear and see how much she loved him. I don't want to change or tarnish that now. But I hope I can be in her life as a friend."

"I think we can work something out once we're safe. She's already taken a fancy to Ben. She told me he cooks so much better than I do, and she loves all his stories."

"My uncle would make a great chef."

"Chef?"

"Yeah, because his dishes are a delicious creation even with something simple like meatloaf." He covered the few steps to her. "How's your migraine?"

"Getting better. The caffeine in the coffee has helped, but I should try to get some more sleep. I've lost so much since the Mederos case landed in my lap."

"C'mon. I'll walk you to your room. I'm going to check upstairs and make sure it's locked down."

"Didn't you do it earlier?"

"Yes, but it doesn't hurt to double- then triple-check. This is when I wish I had a castle turret with only one way inside, guarded by me. If I were a criminal, I'd try the second floor. So many people don't secure windows above the first level."

"In my job as a DA, I've always been cautious, but not like what you're describing."

He took her hand and started for the stairs. "When I walk into a room, I assess it and search for all the ways out. I place myself in the best location to escape and guard my back."

She stopped in the middle of the staircase and turned to him. "How's your life now different from when you were a soldier?"

"There are similarities if you want to stay alive. Even with precautions, a person can be caught off guard like driving to the ranch the night we wrecked. I can't see all possibilities all the time. That's when I give it to the Lord. He's my backup."

With all Cade had been through, he still leaned on God while she was struggling with her faith and why God allowed men like Mederos to win. "Have you ever been shot?"

"Once in the Middle East. That day my buddy was killed, a bullet nicked me. Could have been worse, but I reacted fast. When I went into law enforcement, I had a few close calls but nothing more than a few bruises and cuts."

"So now I've got to add worrying about you to my list."

"No," He cupped her face, his eyes skimming over it. "Worrying is a waste of time and energy. It doesn't change a thing and can only add stress. You don't need another person to worry over."

How did he get to be so wise? She knew he was right, but that didn't make it easy to follow his advice. Worrying came naturally to her. "I'm a mother. It's hard not to."

"You've done a good job with Michelle. She's leveled headed."

"She has her moments. Although her emotions can rule sometimes when they shouldn't. She's fourteen and counting the days until she turns fifteen. Don't you remember how it was to be a teenager? Especially now that she's discovered boys."

His hand slipping to his side, he chuckled. "I like the idea of a castle turret more and more, with a moat around it and alligators in the water. Lots of them."

"You'd have a rebellion on your hands. She is strong-minded."

"Is that another way of saying stubborn?"

She nodded, missing the feel of his hand, more than she had realized. His touch sparked memories of their times together as teens. She'd known when he decided to go into the army after the 9/11 attacks and she went to college that it would be hard for them to grab time together. So when they saw each other between long absences, all their feelings would pour out. Intense. All consuming.

They continued up the stairs.

Cade paused at the bedroom across from Tory's. "Michelle's sleeping in here. This is my office, but it has a daybed as well as some of the boxes I haven't unpacked yet. She didn't mind and kind of liked having her own room." He quietly opened the door and whispered, "I'm going to check her window."

While he crossed to it, Tory moved over to the bed and looked at her daughter, peacefully sleeping as though someone wasn't after them. *Why, Lord? Why is she in danger?* A tear slipped from her eye and coursed down her cheek.

Cade touched her arm and motioned toward the hallway.

She ducked her head and swiped her hand across her face. She had to be strong. For Michelle.

At the bedroom Tory was staying in, she turned to him. "Tomorrow I should be much better, and I can help you by going through my files. They might trigger something not written down that I remember in connection to the people I put away. I'll check the window and make sure it's locked. Thanks for the coffee."

He smiled. "You're welcome. Sleep well. And know that Uncle Ben and I are taking care of you and Michelle."

When she went in and closed the door, she leaned against it, her eyes sliding closed. In her mind's eye, she saw Cade's grin and the laugh lines at the sides of his eyes. His face transformed when he smiled. Flutters in her stomach made a mockery of her declaration that there was nothing between her and Cade anymore.

Cade's eyes burned from all the hours he'd spent staring at a piece of paper on the computer screen. He felt he was no closer discovering who would be after Tory and Michelle than he was yesterday when he started going through the trial cases.

"That frown must mean no good leads."

Cade glanced up at his uncle coming into the dining room from the kitchen. "Pedro Mederos is still our best lead, but according to Paul Drake he's disappeared. When they went to pick him up, he was gone and no one has seen him for thirty hours or so they said."

"As if the kid knew his prints were found on the van. Interesting."

"Yep, as I was interviewing Mederos, two police officers went to bring Pedro in for questioning. They searched all last night and today. Still no sign of him."

"How's Mederos taking this news?"

"Like nothing unusual has happened." Cade sighed. "This makes me wonder if there's a mole at the police department."

"Or the boy did it and fled right after that."

"True. But every law enforcement officer in a two-hundred-mile radius is looking for the teen."

Uncle Ben leaned against the doorjamb, his arms loosely crossed. "There are a lot of places for him to hide. I'm sure Mederos has resources. He could be out of the country by now."

"Paul checked with border patrol. They're on lookout for him." But Cade kept wondering if there was a mole in the department. Mederos usually was one step ahead of the police. "Where are Tory and Michelle? It's been awfully quiet since lunch."

Uncle Ben chuckled. "As opposed to Michelle storming out of the kitchen when she found out she wasn't going to school tomorrow."

"I think the whole house shook when my—Michelle slammed her bedroom door." He had to remember not to let slip Michelle was his daughter, but being so exhausted from trying to figure out who was behind the judge's murder and Tory's break-in, it was easy to forget. For years in his mind he'd referred to Michelle as his daughter. Old habits were hard to stop. "I need a break. I think I have something that might help keep her entertained."

"Yeah, please come up with something. I'm the one who'll be with her most of the day tomorrow."

Cade headed for the back door. "You can regale her with all your stories. In her mind, I'm the one who is keeping her from going to school. I'll be at the barn."

For the next half an hour, he took down the basketball hoop and put it up in the barn. In there Michelle could play to her heart's content. The doors could be bolted from the inside, and with one person guarding her, she should be all right.

He whistled as he made his way back to the house. This should appease her and give her something to do physically. Cade came around to the front of his home and stopped to talk with Deputy Rodriquez. The young man put down the binoculars he used to scan the terrain and greeted Cade.

"Anything?" Cade picked them up and did his own sweep of his ranch.

"A few birds flying overhead, but otherwise nothing has stirred out here. But inside sparks are flying. At least now it's quieted down a little."

Cade thrust the binoculars into the deputy's hand and hurried toward the front door. As he entered, he heard Michelle shouting, "I'm on house arrest. I didn't do anything wrong."

Cade came into the living room in time to see his daughter stamp her foot. "What's going on here?"

Standing by the dining room table with a file in hand, Tory frowned, her shoulders stiff, one arm rigid at her side. "Michelle is arguing about staying here. She insists school is safe, and she would be fine. But mostly she's worried about missing basketball practice."

Cade fixed his undivided attention on Michelle and waited until she looked at him. "I've got something to show you in the barn. It might make this situation a little more bearable."

"I'm one of the best shooters on my team. They need me to win. I don't see anything making this better."

"Fine. If you want to see what I set up, I'll take you. But if you don't, that's okay too." Cade started for the kitchen, needing a tall glass of sweet tea.

Right before he went through the doorway, Michelle said, "Okay. I'll take a look. Anything to break up this boredom. I can't believe you don't have a TV."

"Don't have much time for it, and I certainly don't see that changing any time soon. We'll go in a minute." Cade continued into the kitchen, poured his tea and downed half of it.

When he returned to the living room, both Tory and Michelle were waiting by the door. He looked at Tory. "Getting a little stir-crazy too?"

"Something like that."

Nothing in her expression gave away what she was thinking. Was she worried he'd say something to Michelle about who he was? The mix-up in the past had been cleared up, but it had been obvious their love hadn't been as strong as they had once thought. Once as a teenager, his world had revolved around Tory. The only time he had really argued with her was when he wanted to sign up for the army. He did what he felt he had to do, but their relationship began to fall apart with time and distance. Derek had been here to pick up the pieces. He hadn't.

As they strolled toward the barn, Michelle hurried her pace. "Do you have any horses? I love horses."

"Yes, but they're out to pasture. Horses are only kept in the barn if they're sick or the weather is bad."

"Oh," his daughter murmured, slowing down to a crawl as though there wasn't any other reason to go into the building. "Then why are we coming out here? Do you have other animals in there?"

"There are a couple of stray cats that hang around and keep the mice population down. Also a mixed-breed dog that wandered onto the ranch last summer and has decided to stay. Uncle Ben named him Buddy. He likes to stay outdoors most of the time. Comes to the house only to be fed and see Bella from time to time. I'm pretty sure he's the father to her soon-to-be puppies." Cade scanned the area the whole way to the barn.

He hoped this solution would satisfy Michelle. The ranch was much easier to defend, with its flat terrain and not much in the way of a hiding place for three or four hundred yards around his house. He reached the door, unlocked it and swung it wide, then went in first, giving a quick sweep of the barn's interior.

Behind him Michelle exclaimed, "You moved the hoop. Why?"

"I thought it would be safer for you when you want to shoot hoops. You can practice in here so long as someone is with you—the deputy, Uncle Ben or myself. In fact, I'd love to shoot with you. It's been years, so I'm hoping it's like riding a bicycle. Once I start again, it'll all come back to me."

"You want to play now? Mom can't hit a hoop if her life de…" Michelle snapped her mouth closed, the color fading from her face. "I mean Mom prefers watching rather than playing."

"That's because you've got talent. I don't. I'm a great cheerleader so you two play." Tory shared a look with Cade that warmed him.

He remembered those times she would watch him play and cheered for him. That was when life was much simpler. He walked into the tack room and retrieved the only basketball that had air in it. When he came out, he tossed it to Michelle. "Let's play one-on-one. You keep time, Tory. Thirty minutes."

For the next half an hour the score remained close until Michelle made a shot and Tory shouted, "Time."

Cade grinned. "You're good. You take after your father."

Holding the ball, Michelle smiled from ear to ear. "That's what Mom says. He was a great teacher. Thanks for fixing this up." She headed to the tack room with the basketball.

Cade swiped the back of his forearm across his forehead. "Never thought that would ever happen."

Tory's expression transformed from a grin into a pensive look, her eyes darkening.

He covered the distance to her, glanced at the tack room and whispered, "I told you I won't say anything to Michelle, and I'll keep my word, but I'd like to have more opportunities like this with her."

As Michelle returned, Tory nodded. "Thanks." Then to her daughter she said, "I don't know about you, but I worked up an appetite watching you guys play. Ben is fixing beef stew for dinner. Let's see if we can eat a little early."

"I'm game," Michelle said, a smile still lighting her face.

Cade followed them to the house. As they entered, his cell phone rang. He checked the number, but didn't recognize it. He paused and let Tory and Michelle go into the living room before he answered it. "Morgan here."

"I'm being framed. I didn't kill the judge."

"Is this Pedro Mederos?"

"Yes."

"Where are you?"

"Someplace you won't find me, but you're being played."

Then the connection went dead. Cade looked up.

Tory stood in the entrance to the living room, watching him. "Bad news?"

"It was Pedro Mederos telling me he didn't kill Judge Parks."

"Do you believe him?"

"Let's say I'm keeping an open mind. It seemed mighty convenient that his fingerprint was found on the handle of the tailgate of the truck as though someone wants us to tie the judge's murder to Mederos."

"But sometimes the criminals aren't smart. Pedro isn't savvy like his brother. He could have made that mistake in the passion of the murder."

"And go against what his brother wanted?"

"You only have Mederos's word that he didn't tell his gang to go after Judge Parks. I can see him doing whatever he needs to do to get off. Terrorizing others is a tactic he uses a lot."

He cut the space between them. "We'll get to the bottom of this. You and Michelle aren't safe until then, so I have a lot at stake."

"I'm not sure what would have happened if you hadn't stepped forward. Your ranch is the perfect place for us to stay. And the chance to practice basketball hopefully will make it bearable for Michelle. She doesn't always make good decisions."

"What teen does? I can remember a few we made."

She grinned. "Just a few?"

"Okay, more than a few."

"Cade, Michelle wasn't one of them."

"I agree. I've enjoyed getting to know her."

"What if things had been different fifteen years ago? Have you ever wondered that?"

"Sure." A lot more than he wanted to admit, especially since he'd returned to El Rio. He'd even played the "what-if" game. What if he hadn't gone into the army after 9/11? What if he hadn't been sent away on a secret mission for months?

"So have I. Especially lately."

He inched closer, drawn to her. Part of him was surprised. It must be the close quarters they were keeping. He was around her a lot lately.

No matter how much he told himself it wouldn't work between them. Their past was a huge barrier to any relationship. And then there was Michelle. The more he was around her, the more he wanted to be in her life.

"We should talk again when this is over with," he murmured close to her, his eyes trained on her mouth.

He wanted to kiss her. He shouldn't, but she lifted her chin and their gazes connected. He leaned closer, his heart revving into overdrive. His lips grazed like a whisper over hers.

FIVE

Tory wanted Cade to kiss her. She could still remember how it had felt years ago. His lips brushed across hers. His scent surrounded her, flinging her back to the time they used to go horseback riding, relishing every moment together.

"Mom. Cade." The sound of approaching footsteps jerked her back to the present.

Tory put several feet between her and Cade as Michelle walked through the living room to them.

"Ben has dinner on the table." Michelle shifted her gaze between them, her forehead scrunching. "Is something wrong?"

The heat of Tory's blush couldn't fade fast enough. "No." She headed for the kitchen, at a loss for words. How much had Michelle seen?

"Your mother was soothing my bruised ego after losing to you at basketball."

"You didn't *let* me win, did you?" her daughter asked.

"No way. It was fair and square."

"Good. I'll never get better if you let me win."

"I might have to practice before I play you again." Michelle giggled.

Tory hadn't heard that sound much lately. It was good to hear in the middle of everything that was going on.

"I've been telling Ben about how I creamed you," Michelle said as she came into the kitchen a couple of paces ahead of Cade.

He laughed. "Creamed me? I hardly call winning by two points a defeat. Next time I'll show you what creaming someone is."

Ben placed the bowl of beef stew in the middle of the table. "I can see I'm gonna have to referee the game."

"Do you play basketball?" Michelle took Ben's hand and Cade's.

"Who do you think taught your dad—and Cade how?" Ben ducked his head and began to say grace.

Tory's heart thumped. The near slip illustrated how easy it was to let down her guard. She added a short, silent plea at the end of the blessing. Michelle needed to be protected not just physically but also emotionally.

After the medical examiner gave his testimony, Judge Duggin, the new judge assigned to the trial, dismissed court for the day. Tory glanced at her watch and noted the time was a little earlier than yesterday. After a long, tension-filled day, she was glad to leave. Twisting around in her chair, she caught sight of Cade sitting at the back of the courtroom. He smiled, and suddenly she didn't feel so tired. His presence lifted her spirits.

When she talked with Michelle at lunch today, she'd wanted to know how the trial was going. If her daughter had her wish, the case would be over as soon as possible. She felt like she was letting down her basketball team because they were playing tonight without her. Tory wanted it over with, but the defense attorney was dragging things out. The only reason she could think of was that Mederos's men hadn't discovered the star witness's location.

Cade met her halfway down the center aisle, nodding at Officer Sims, who was her guard, then asked her, "How did it go?"

"Tedious. The defense questioned every finding the ME gave. All I want to do is get out of here. How about your day?"

"Still searching for Pedro Mederos. Every lead is a dead end. I'm beginning to believe the teen really is far away from here. When is your star witness going to testify?"

"Hopefully in a couple of days. We have some other witnesses subpoenaed to testify first."

Cade opened the courtroom door and stepped out first, panning the hallway before signaling her to leave. Officer Sims followed behind her as they made their way to the exit closest to the parking lot. Cade had left the new car he was using in a spot as near to the door as possible. But there was still twenty feet to cover.

Tory didn't breathe until she slid into the front passenger seat. The vehicle Cade was using for transporting her to and from the ranch was bulletproof. One would also be used for the star witness. The state wanted Mederos convicted, and this was their best shot at doing it.

But she couldn't wait to have her life back.

As she waved goodbye to her police guard, Cade started the SUV and pulled out of the parking lot. "Detective Alexander has exhausted any leads from the forensics collected at your house. There are latent prints in the bathroom, but they don't match anyone in the system, which doesn't help us right now."

"At the trial they'll help convict the intruder."

"If we can find who they match."

"So we don't know who broke in or for that matter why."

"No. Members of the biker gang I talked to earlier today insisted it wasn't them who trashed your house and killed the judge. The ones whose fingerprints are on record didn't match what was in your house so there wasn't much we could do there."

"Now that's a surprise they didn't confess." Tory tried to keep a straight face, but a grin teased the corners of her mouth.

"Actually when I talked to them, there wasn't anything in their body language to indicate they were lying."

"I imagine they've had a lot of practice at lying."

"True, but something doesn't feel right with all that's been going on. What's been happening just keeps raising more questions. Did Pedro kill Judge Parks or did someone set him up as he and his brother say? If so, why did that person do it? What is his objective? I feel like there's something else occurring here or there is more than one plan in play."

"So you think Mederos and his brother are telling the truth about Judge Parks?"

Cade stopped at the intersection leading to the highway. "Trashing your house and taking those photos might not be connected to the judge's murder. I have to look at all possibilities."

"We have to. I have a big stake in this. My daughter's life is in danger."

"*Our* daughter."

Tory nodded, closing her eyes. "It'll be good to return to the ranch." The realization she meant every word took her by surprise. When did her feelings start changing? For years, she'd been angry at Cade and felt betrayed. Now she couldn't quite pinpoint what she was feeling.

She released a long calming breath as they approached Cade's two-story adobe house. "I hope Ben hasn't been pulling his hair out while trying to get Michelle to do her schoolwork."

"I doubt it. With me he used to be a regular drill sergeant. Not much got past him."

The second the SUV pulled up to Cade's home, Michelle flew out the front door and nearly leaped down the porch steps. "I'm finished with my assignments. Let's go play basketball," she announced as Cade climbed from the car.

Poor Ben. He had to contain all that energy today. Tory exited the vehicle and greeted the deputy sheriff on duty seconds before Michelle grabbed her hand and tugged her toward the barn. "Hold it. Let us go inside, put our stuff up and get something to drink."

"But I've been inside all day. A gal has to have fresh air."

Cade came up behind them and hooked his arm around each one's shoulder. "C'mon. I need to change into some workout clothes because I intend to stomp all over you."

"In your dreams," Michelle said with a laugh.

"This sounds serious. I hope Ben will referee." Tory mounted the steps, so glad her daughter had something to look forward to.

Cade's uncle swung the door wide and stood in the entrance. "She's been waiting at the door the last half an hour." Then as Michelle entered first, Ben leaned close to Tory and whispered, "Promising she'd shoot hoops was the only way I could get her to do her schoolwork."

"You'll deserve a medal when this is over with. Thanks for watching her, Ben."

"Anytime." Then in a lower tone he added, "I see a lot of her father in her."

That comment stayed with Tory while she changed into jeans, tennis shoes and a T-shirt. The more she saw Cade and Michelle together, the more similarities she discovered—the way they tilted their head when listening to someone or the way a smile took over their whole expression. But mostly when she looked at Cade's eyes, the resemblance was so obvious—more than she had originally thought. Would her daughter ever notice? Would others when Cade and Michelle were side by side?

In the kitchen Tory grabbed a bottle of water from the refrigerator, then shut the door. When she turned, three sets of eyes were on her.

"Mom, you are so slow. Good thing you don't play basketball."

"It's been a long day, but I'm ready now."

On the trek to the barn Cade kept up with Michelle while Ben walked with Tory, thankfully at a much slower pace. "I wish I had her energy."

"I know what you mean. In desperation, I let her dribble the ball in the kitchen when she took a break from her schoolwork. And thankfully Bella helped the situation until I had to let her outside."

"Michelle isn't used to being so confined."

"I had to resort to taking her cell phone away when I kept catching her reading texts from her friends. I wonder if any of them were listening to their teachers."

"She has the ability to text while looking right at you."

"These kids' skill sets today are so different from when I was growing up."

"The world is rapidly changing."

While Cade unlocked the front barn door and swung it wide, Michelle darted inside.

Seconds later, a scream chilled the air.

Tory froze.

Cade ran inside.

Ben grabbed Tory's arm and rushed toward the barn.

When she entered the dimly lit interior, her gaze fixed on Michelle, standing in front of the hoop. An inflatable plastic woman hung dangling from a rope tied around its neck. Tory hurried forward and hugged her daughter. Michelle shook in the circle of her arms.

Words of solace fled Tory's mind as she stared at a photo of her entering the courtroom this morning attached to the chest of the life-size plastic doll. She fought to keep from shuddering, but she couldn't stop the fear from washing over her.

They know where we are.

"You all need to get back to the house. Wait just a second." Cade took out his cell phone and snapped pictures of the hanging doll, then strode to the trio near the exit. He tossed his keys to his uncle. "Bring the SUV around. I don't want them exposed any more than they have to be."

As Ben loped over to the car, Cade shielded them

with his body and kept his attention riveted to their surroundings.

Tory held Michelle, sure that her daughter felt the hammering of her heartbeat against her chest. It was bad enough that Michelle saw her trashed bedroom and the bathroom, but this was far worse. Someone wanted them to realize there was nowhere they would be safe. A taunt, and plainly a threat against Tory.

Cade opened the two doors so Ben could drive the car into the barn. Once everyone was in the vehicle, Ben backed out and headed for the house.

He pulled up to the back door. "The deputy is checking the house, then we can go inside."

When the young man came outside and gave the all-clear signal, Ben ushered Tory into the house while Cade escorted Michelle.

The second her daughter was safe, Michelle wrenched away from them. "He was in the barn. He hung that," Michelle flapped one arm in anger and fear, "that *thing* to scare us. This wasn't supposed to happen."

"I'm sorry, honey." Helplessness attacked Tory.

"I hate your job," Michelle screamed, running from the kitchen with Cade's pregnant dog following her.

Tory didn't know what to say to Michelle because right now she had no control over what was happening. She started to follow Michelle.

Cade stepped into her path. "I'll know more when I go back and check the barn. I'll call Paul and the sheriff to let them know. Give her time to calm down. She won't hear what you're saying right now."

"Michelle is my daughter. I know her better than you." Her own anger came to the foreground, and she went after Michelle. She had to try to talk to her. Cade had no idea what Tory had been going through the past few years after Derek's death. Her even-tempered daughter's emotions were all over the place. She realized it was partly due to Michelle's age, but her life had been rocked to the core when Derek unexpectedly died from a heart attack at such a young age.

Tory knocked on the closed door. When Michelle didn't say come in, Tory tried the handle. The door was locked. She pounded on it, but Michelle didn't say anything. Panic surged in her.

Then she heard a sob through the wooden barrier. Michelle might be physically safe, but she wasn't emotionally all right.

Tory hadn't planned for any of this, and she didn't know how to deal with it. *God, where are You? I need You.*

The sound of footsteps coming up the staircase made Tory stiffen. She didn't want to see anyone. She swung around to hurry to her room when Cade poked his head around the corner.

She stopped, the compassion in his expression releasing a flood of emotions she'd tried to dam. He covered the distance in several long strides and gathered her into his arms.

"She's shut me out."

He nodded his head toward the staircase. "Let's go downstairs and talk."

"That's not going to help. Finding the person doing all of this will."

He captured her against his side and moved to the steps, whispering, "Do you want Michelle to overhear us?"

She shook her head.

In the living room, she sat at one end of the couch with Cade at the other while Ben took the chair across from them.

Cade moved closer until there was nothing between them. "Remember that time you were angry with your mother because she wouldn't let you go to the school dance, and she tried to talk with you. You wouldn't listen. She kept pressing and you two had a big fight. Give Michelle the time your mother should have given you that day to calm down."

"Michelle blames me for all of this."

"She's upset and saying whatever comes to mind." Cade held her hand between his. "I'm meeting Detective Alexander and Sheriff Dawson in the barn. The deputy is over there to make sure no one goes in until it's been processed."

"Why did someone leave that in the barn?"

"To throw us off our game."

"No. He can't get to me, so he wants me to know he's still after me but also Michelle."

"I won't let that happen, Tory." He squeezed her hand gently. "We'll talk more when I've checked the barn."

Cade walked out the front door. Tory's feelings were conflicted. Part of her wanted to go hide and pull herself together by herself. But she also didn't want to be alone with her problems either. How could a person want two opposing things at the same time?

"Tory, He's with you," Ben said across from her, his aging face solemn. But there was a light in his eyes. "You aren't going through this by yourself. Turn to Him and draw strength."

"I know Cade is doing everything he can, but even *he* can't promise Michelle's safety."

"I wasn't talking about my nephew although he will do all he can to keep that promise. I'm talking about the Lord. A lot has happened to you in a short amount of time. You don't even have time to recover from one blow before another strikes you. But God is with you, supporting you."

"Everything I'm trying isn't working. I feel like my life has totally fallen apart. My daughter doesn't want me to be a DA and I understand why, but I feel this is what I'm supposed to do. Helping to keep El Rio safe."

"If that's your path, then there will be other ways to keep El Rio safe or you're meant to be where you are. Turn to God. Ask Him. Turn your future over to Him. I discovered that the hard way. I used to fight His plan every step, and it was an exhausting battle. When I finally gave control to Him, He astounded me."

His words made sense, but could she put them into practice? "Thanks, Ben. You've given me something to think about. But I need to do something about Michelle."

"We could always remove the furniture in here and hang a hoop up in the living room."

The image brought a chuckle from Tory.

"I'm half serious if it'll keep her calm and not thinking about what's going on. Or maybe Bella will hurry up and have her puppies. That will keep her attention for a little while." He smiled. "Remember how you were at fourteen. Put yourself in her shoes. And give her time. You've done a good job of raising her."

It didn't feel like it at the moment. "You can be my uncle anytime." Tory pushed to her feet. "I'm going to get ready for bed."

As she climbed the stairs, she realized she had a lot

to consider. It was times like this that she missed her parents and their guidance. But mostly she missed the connection she used to have with the Lord. Her life had been so busy the past few years that she'd moved away from Him. Her first priority would be spending quiet time with God every day and reconnecting.

Cade shook Detective Anderson's hand. "It's good to see you. I know this is out of your jurisdiction, but since it's connected to the incident at Tory's house, I thought you needed to be brought in. Sheriff Dawson got called away and will come out here later to look around."

"Tell me what happened." Anderson took his own pictures while Cade went through how he discovered the hanging plastic doll. "The intruder got into the barn by cutting the chains I had locked around the back door handles."

"Did you touch anything?"

"No."

"Then I'll take fingerprints and see if I have any usable ones, especially on the inflatable woman."

"Maybe we'll get a break and what we find will match with someone's in the system."

"When was the last time you were in here before this happened?" Alexander pointed to the dummy dangling from a rope.

"We played basketball last evening before dark. No one at the ranch came in here after that."

"So we're talking almost twenty-four hours. We had footage from traffic cams for the two directions a person can drive their car toward Tory's house. Let me see what we can get from the last camera leaving town on this highway and see if there are any matches. It's a long shot. At Tory's house the intruder very likely didn't drive to her place. Some criminals make dumb mistakes, but it's not too hard to if he wanted to avoid being captured on the traffic cam near her house."

"I know it'll take time to go through the tapes and it's a long shot, but no one on the street reported anyone suspicious in Tory's neighborhood during the time frame."

"What if they're afraid to say something?" The detective jotted a note on his pad.

"That's possible considering the members of the biker gang are our main suspects. But a lot of the neighbors work and wouldn't be home at that time. I'll find out from Tory who might have been around and pay them another visit tomorrow. I've finished talking with Mederos's cohorts, at least the ones I could find."

"Since I haven't heard anything, I'm assuming you got nothing."

"You assumed right. One way or another his trial will probably be over next week."

"And you think the harassment will stop then."

Cade shrugged. "I hope so."

"What if Tory's daughter was the real target of the trashing and photos? What's happening to her may have nothing to do with Judge Parks's murder. Have you considered that?"

"Yes and I'm still considering it. I'm looking at each incident as separate and yet possibly connected." Cade hated leaving Tory after Michelle's reaction to this latest taunt. "Do you need me for anything else?"

"No. I'll take the plastic doll down and see if I can track where it came from. I'll look around on my own.

Have you checked the whole barn to make sure nothing else is in here that shouldn't be?"

"No, only a cursory inspection. My priority is keeping Tory and Michelle safe so I wanted to get them away from the barn as fast as possible."

"I understand."

"If you find anything, let me know or take a photo and show me before you leave. I don't want to be gone too long." Cade left the detective taking photos of the back door.

He didn't have high hopes of Alexander finding anything that would lead to the culprit. A more pressing concern was making sure Michelle had calmed down. This was not the time to rebel.

When he entered his house, the first thing he noticed was the silence. The second was the scent of pizza. His uncle made them from scratch, and they were delicious. Cade grinned. Uncle Ben was a wise man. Michelle's favorite food was pizza with everything but anchovies on it.

He made his way into the kitchen. "Where's Tory?"

"She's in her bedroom."

"Was she all right after I left to meet Detective Alexander?"

"Better but not all right. I have a feeling that isn't gonna happen until she knows Michelle will be safe."

"I know what Tory's feeling."

Uncle Ben turned off the oven. "I'll keep these warm. See if you can get Tory and Michelle to come down to eat. I was hoping the smell might draw your daugh— sorry, Michelle out of her locked room."

"You've got to be careful. Her life right now is so

fragile. I don't want to add anything to what's going on in Michelle's life."

"No one has asked, but how are you doing with them here, especially Michelle?"

"I'm fine. So long as I can keep them alive."

"Have you and Tory forgiven each other?"

Had they? "I haven't taken the time to consider if I have. But—" Cade cocked his head to the side "—I think I have. I can't answer for Tory."

"It's a start. Go tell them dinner is ready." His uncle took the plates and utensils to the table.

"Will do."

Cade climbed the stairs two at a time. The scent of the crust baking along with the various toppings had stirred his hunger. When he knocked on Tory's bedroom door, she almost answered it immediately.

"I was just about ready to come down. Ben knows how to torture a person. I didn't eat much at lunch, and I'm starving."

"Me too."

Tory glanced at Michelle's closed door. "I'll let Michelle know it's ready. It'll be hard for her to turn down pizza, but I won't be surprised if she does. I haven't seen her this upset since Derek's death." She started for their daughter's room.

Cade moved quickly, catching her arm and halting her. "Let me talk to her. Sometimes it can work better in this kind of situation if a relative stranger talks to her." He didn't want to be a stranger to her. He didn't want yesterday's basketball game to be the only one they ever had.

"I don't know if that's…" Tory stared into his eyes. "Please."

She blinked and looked away. "Okay. But don't expect too much."

"I won't." All he could do was hope. He'd counseled troubled teens he'd encountered in his job, but not one that was his child—and didn't know it. He felt like he stood at the edge of a hot lava flow and what he sought was trapped in the middle.

He knocked on Michelle's door.

"Mom, go away. I don't want to talk. I don't want dinner."

"Michelle, it's Cade. Can I come in?" He hadn't tried the handle to see if it was locked as before. He needed her to open the door because she wanted to talk to him. He wouldn't use the master key. Forcing her to listen wouldn't work. It never had for him as he was growing up.

The minutes ticked by. How long should he stay? What in the world was he going to say to make the situation better? Why did he think he could?

The lock turned, and the door opened. Michelle grasped the frame as though it were the only thing holding her up. Her red-rimmed eyes lifted to his. Bella moseyed out of the bedroom and headed toward the stairs.

"I wish I had the right words to make this all go away, but I don't. But I'm a good listener if you need someone to talk to."

She let him in. "I wish Dad was here."

"I miss Derek too."

"And now Mom is in danger. Why does she want to prosecute bad guys?"

"Why do you think?"

Tears filled up her blue eyes—eyes so much like his.

She rubbed them and turned away. "Because her friend was killed in a bank robbery."

"That's what motivated her to become a prosecutor, but I think now there are other reasons why she stays in the job. El Rio is growing fast because of its location, and so has the crime rate, but she's working to keep that down and is succeeding. The conviction rate since she took office has increased. That's a good thing."

"Not if someone wants her dead. I know that picture was taken today. She had on that outfit when she came home earlier. Someone is following her."

"I was right beside her when that picture was snapped. It was taken at a distance."

"I know the kind of things Mederos has done. Some people have disappeared and haven't been found. Others…" Shivering, Michelle hugged herself.

"Where did you hear this?"

"I saw it online. Is it true?"

"I don't know exactly what you read, but Mederos is a criminal who needs to be brought to justice. He doesn't care who he hurts to get what he wants. Your mom is trying to stop him once and for all."

"Why can't someone else do it?"

"I'm going to do all I can to make sure she stays safe. You too."

"Because it's your job?"

"Yes." *And because you're my daughter.*

"What if you can't?"

"I don't think in can'ts but in cans. As someone once said, failure isn't an option."

Michelle stuck out her lower lip. "I still want Mom to quit. Then we'll be safe."

If only it were that simple. "Right now, all I can

think about is how hungry I am. Wait till you have my uncle's pizza."

"I'm not..." Her stomach suddenly growled in hunger. She giggled. "Well, maybe I am hungry."

"C'mon, let's eat."

She looked around as though she wasn't sure she should leave the room.

"I can bring a plate up to you, if you want, but then you'd miss hearing how Uncle Ben decided he could make better pizza than the joint in town that everyone loves."

"He can? I love that place."

When they entered the kitchen, Uncle Ben and Tory sat at the table, their heads bowed as his uncle blessed the food. The second Tory glanced up, the expression of joy in her eyes was all the thanks Cade needed.

Cade sat in the chair across from Michelle. "This smells great."

"Yeah." Michelle grabbed a slice of pizza and took a bite. "This is the best ever. Yours is so much better than Pizza Galore."

Uncle Ben beamed.

As they ate dinner, a sense of family hung in the air. This was what Cade had missed all these years. He only wished there was a way to preserve this feeling, in order to relish it in the lonely days ahead.

The next day, after long, tiring hours in court, Tory gathered her notes and stuffed them into her briefcase. Pushing to her feet, she caught Mederos's gaze boring into her as he was escorted from the courtroom. He was a master at intimidation, but after the plastic doll left in the barn yesterday, her resolve was stronger than ever. He needed to be stopped.

Michelle might not like the idea she couldn't leave Cade's ranch house, but she would be protected while Tory finally put this man in prison for his crimes. She'd make it so uncomfortable for the biker gang that they would move on. Tomorrow the hard part would be over. Carlos Dietz would testify, then disappear into the Witness Protection Program. People would see they could stand up to a man like Mederos and survive. She would be calling Carlos earlier than planned and hoped that would throw a wrench into Mederos's plan of intimidation.

Tory turned away from the sight of Mederos exiting and greeted Cade with a smile. "I'm ready to leave. Any progress with the case of the dummy?"

"Just to clarify. Who or what dummy are you referring to?"

She chuckled. "I wish I could say Mederos was a dummy, but he's smart."

Officer Sims stood on her left side while Cade was on her right. "Even smart ones can be tripped up. It would be nice not to have to deal with the Mederos gang anymore. I'm rooting for you. That's why I volunteered to be the one guarding you in the courtroom."

While putting on a protective vest, Tory slanted a glance at the police officer. "I'm glad you're here. I know the people coming into the courtroom go through security, but half the audience are members of his gang."

"What surprises me is that they're behaving." Officer Sims hit the first floor button on the elevator.

"That's so they won't get kicked out and banned from the courtroom." Cade stepped out into the lobby then signaled for Tory and Officer Sims to follow him toward the back of the building where the reserved parking lot was.

While Cade jogged to the SUV, Tory stayed back with Officer Sims inside near the double door. "Mederos's gang members are there to intimidate the jury, judge and me. You know the saying, if looks could kill, I'd be dead by now."

"Too bad we can't throw them in jail for their thoughts." Officer Sims peered out the glass part of the door. "Morgan has pulled up and is getting out. Ready?"

"Definitely ready to go home and get some rest." The second she said the word home, she was glad Cade hadn't heard her. In the few days she'd spent there, she'd come to feel at home at his ranch. Even the threat left in the barn last night hadn't totally taken that sensation away.

Officer Sims opened one of the double doors, stepped outside and motioned for her to exit the courthouse too while Cade came around the front of the armored SUV.

Her police guard moved closer to her as she strode forward, her gaze trained on Cade. She focused on the strong slant of his jaw, the exhaustion he was trying to hide from her, and realized her feelings concerning him were rekindling.

Crack!

Cade flew toward her, his body slamming into her.

Another crack reverberated through the stillness.

SIX

Cade cushioned Tory as much as he could as they both crashed into the concrete walkway, but the collision forced air from his lungs. No time to process the pain assaulting him, he shielded Tory while drawing his gun and searching their surroundings. The shards of the glass window on the door behind them littered the area.

Officer Sims lay sprawled on the sidewalk, a gunshot hole in the upper part of his chest not covered by his protective vest. He moaned, his eyelids sliding closed.

"Tory, are you all right?" Cade asked her as he looked for the assailant while pulling his cell phone free.

"I—think so," she said as she tried to breathe.

He made a call to 911. "Officer down at the courthouse's north entrance in the reserved parking lot. Need backup and an ambulance. Two shots fired so far."

After reporting the incident, Cade checked the area between him and the car. If they stayed low, the SUV could block another attempt. "I need you to follow me, then I'm coming back to see about Sims."

Wincing, she raised her head and looked at the fallen officer. "Is he alive?"

"I hope so." He lifted off Tory enough to allow her

room to move to a crouching position while still being between her and where he thought the shot might have come from. "There's a rooftop on the building behind the courthouse. The shooter might be there. I'm going to use the armored SUV to shield you. Get inside and stay down."

Her gaze still glued to Sims, she nodded slightly.

Using his body as a buffer, he ran low with Tory behind him to the car. He opened the front door and assisted her inside while the sound of sirens pierced the air as though coming toward them from all directions.

Cade went back to see if he should move Sims closer to the SUV, but when he assessed his position, the officer was hidden from the line of sight from the building behind the parking lot. As Cade felt for a pulse, patrol cars flooded the parking lot, forming a barrier while two paramedics came from the courthouse with a gurney.

"I can't find a pulse," Cade told the EMTs.

Cade moved away to allow them to work on the fallen officer. He shifted his focus to getting Tory out of harm's way. Since the two earlier shots, there hadn't been any more. Most likely the assailant escaped, but even with that in mind, he used the cars as a barrier between him and a possible location of the shooter while he made his way to Chief Paul Drake crouched behind his car and talking on the radio.

"I've got two teams searching the office building. So far nothing but two shell casings on the roof." Paul rose to examine the building behind the courthouse. "How's Tory?"

"She said okay, but everything was crazy."

"Stay with her until we get the area cleared. How's Sims?"

"I don't know. Not good. There were two shots, but he only has one gunshot wound. The second one—" Cade glanced toward the shattered entrance door window into the courthouse "—is I'd say somewhere inside."

Paul watched the two paramedics transfer the police officer to the gurney. "We'll check for it."

Cade headed toward the driver side of the SUV to be ready to take Tory to the ranch as soon as the police chief gave the go-ahead. He quickly slipped behind the steering wheel and looked at Tory crouched between the dashboard and the passenger seat, her head bowed, her left hand clutching her right upper arm.

"Tory, we should be able to leave soon."

As she raised her head, he saw the blood leaking through her fingers.

"The bullet must have grazed me. I didn't realize it at first. It isn't too bad. How's Officer Sims?"

"On his way to the hospital. Like you'll be in a few seconds." Cade called out to Paul and told him to have the patrol cars moved.

Tory thought of sitting in the passenger seat, but the effort to wiggle free of the small space she'd wedged herself in seemed enormous at the moment.

Cade leaned toward her. "Let me see the wound."

When she removed her hand, blood seeped even more from the injury, the red staining her navy blue suit jacket growing. "See, it isn't that bad."

"Stay put. I'll help you when we get to the hospital."

"Good because I wasn't going anywhere." She tried

to make the quip sound light, as though pain wasn't radiating down her arm, but she didn't succeed.

His look of concern deepened as he threw the SUV into drive. She rested her head against the passenger door, remembering the time she'd argued with Cade about wearing a protective vest in the courtroom. She'd wanted to present a confident bearing to the jury. Finally they had agreed she would wear one when she went to and from the courthouse but not while the trial was in session.

Please Lord. Take care of Sims. He was there because of me.

What would she do if something had happened to Cade? Michelle was the only family she had left. She'd lost her parents and husband. She didn't want her daughter to lose Cade even if Michelle never knew who he was.

"We're here." Cade glanced at her, the same expression of worry still in place. "Don't move. I'll come around and help you." When he opened her door, he laid his hand on her back. "I'm going to put my arm around you to assist you. Let me do the work. You protect your injury."

In less than a minute Cade cushioned her against him, then walked slowly toward the emergency room entrance. Her legs wobbled, and Cade practically carried her into the reception lobby. A nurse brought a wheelchair that Tory eased into and started to wheel her away.

"Wait." Tory looked back at Cade. "Don't let Michelle know I was shot. I need to tell her myself." She dreaded that conversation. Her daughter would only keep demanding that she quit her job. She might, but not in the middle of the Mederos trial.

"I won't, but I'm letting Uncle Ben know. He'll have to tell her something when you're late tonight or she'll worry."

What if she had to stay overnight? Michelle would freak if Tory had to, because Derek had died in a hospital.

At midnight Cade pulled up to his ranch house, two deputy sheriffs guarding it now. Tory sighed.

Home, safe at last. The thought stunned her.

After Cade parked in the garage, he looked at Tory, his jacket covering her because hers was ruined. In the dim light, he assessed her.

She closed her eyes in relief. The day could have ended so much worse. "I hope that Michelle is asleep. I'd rather tell her in the morning."

"You'll have a little extra time since the trial won't resume until the afternoon."

"I'm so glad that Officer Sims's surgery was successful."

"He should recover. Stay put. I'm helping you out of the car."

"I can walk into the house by myself. If Michelle's up—"

Hand on his door handle, Cade frowned. "You're weak from blood loss. This isn't up for discussion."

"Fine. I don't have enough energy to argue with you, but I'm walking inside on my own."

He muttered something about difficult women under his breath and climbed from the SUV. If she wasn't so tired, she would've smiled.

When Cade opened her door, he leaned in to support her weight as she rose from the seat. "See, this isn't so bad."

His close proximity sped her heart up. She could smell his coffee-laced breath. When his arm went around her to hold her against him, she couldn't seem to breathe in enough oxygen. Afraid she would become lightheaded, she forced deep gulps of air into her lungs.

The door to the kitchen crashed open, and Michelle stood in the entryway. "What's taken you…" Her words sputtered to a halt, her eyes growing round as she took in her mother against Cade, one of his jackets around her. "What's wrong?"

"Let's get inside, and your mom will tell you everything." Cade moved forward, whispering to Tory while her daughter backed away, "Sorry Michelle is up."

"I probably won't sleep worrying about tomorrow anyway, so I might as well get this over with." Tory mounted the step into the kitchen and disengaged from Cade. "Let's go into the living room where it's comfortable." She shrugged off the jacket slowly and handed it to Cade.

When Michelle's gaze lit upon the white bandage around her upper arm, Tory hadn't thought her daughter's eyes could get any wider. But they looked like giant saucers, along with her mouth opening and closing silently, like a fish.

As Tory slowly made her way to the living room and sat on the couch, she tried to come up with the best way to tell Michelle what happened. *Please, God, give me the right words.*

Michelle took the chair across from her while Cade sat next to Tory. He covered her hand on the couch between them and gently squeezed it. She wasn't alone. He was here. Some of the worry melted away. She was alive. Officer Sims was too. She was thankful for that.

Michelle opened her mouth, and Tory immediately cut her off. "When I left the courthouse today, there was a shooting. I was nicked in the arm. The doctor said I would be fine. If it had been serious, he would have kept me in the hospital." She glanced at Cade. "He was there to protect me and keep me safe."

Michelle's gaze bored into Cade. "Not safe enough. You were shot."

"None of this is his fault or mine, for that matter. I wish I could protect you forever from the evil in this world, but I can't."

"But you could have been killed."

"Yes, I could have but I wasn't. I'm learning I can't dwell on what-ifs and maybes. If I worry about every possibility, I would become paralyzed with fear. I refuse to live like that, afraid to do the right thing, afraid to live my life for what I was meant to do. I feel the Lord wants me to fight evil the way I know best, through the law." Again she threw a look at Cade. "He fights it by being a law enforcement officer. If no one stepped up to do those jobs, evil would win. I won't let that happen. Ever." She turned her hand over and clasped his, the warmth of his palm against hers calming.

Michelle's eyes filled with tears. "But what if I lose you?"

"There's always that possibility no matter what I do. Don't let fear rule you, or you'll never live up to your potential."

Her daughter swung her attention from her to Cade then to Ben. "You sound just like Ben. I knew something was wrong, but he wouldn't tell me. In fact, he said very little."

"That's because I asked him not to. I wanted to be the one to do that."

Ben's cheeks reddened. "I won't lie, which meant I didn't say much."

Michelle rose and came over to Tory, leaning down to kiss her on the cheek. "Then I won't lie. I don't know if I can do what you want, but I'll try. I'm going to bed."

Tory waited until she heard the sounds of her daughter's footsteps fading as she moved up the stairs. "What have you done with Michelle? She didn't fall apart like I thought she would."

"She asked me how come I wasn't worried about my nephew. I told her my worrying wouldn't change anything other than stress me out, then I challenged her to a chess game. She's good."

"Derek taught her. It's good she found someone to play with. I have no idea how to."

Cade stiffened for a few seconds, then relaxed again. "He was a good father to her."

Her gaze met his. "Yes."

"I'm glad. It makes me feel better about what happened all those years ago."

Ben rose and walked to the entrance into the living room, glancing toward the staircase. "Okay, before you two go to bed, tell me what really happened today. I wanted to listen to my police scanner, but I couldn't."

"After the gunshot, things are fuzzy for me. When Cade tackled me, I hit the ground so hard the breath was knocked from my lungs. I don't think the whole incident took more than ten minutes, but for most of that

I was hunkering down in the car." She waved her hand at Cade. "You've got the stage. I'd like to know too."

Cade recapped what happened from the first shot to the drive to the hospital.

"What are Officer Sims's chances of recovering?" Ben asked as he paced from one end of the room to the other.

"Good. He shouldn't have to stay in the hospital long." Cade lounged back and laid his arm along the couch behind Tory. "I know you, Uncle Ben. What are you thinking?"

"Did the first shot hit Tory and the second the officer?"

Tory tried to replay the brief scene in her head, but her mind was fuzzy. "I don't know. What do you think, Cade?"

"I was in react mode, but I don't remember seeing the gunshot hitting Sims so it might have been the second one. So you think Officer Sims was the target?"

"Maybe. Of course, you were probably blocking Tory by that time, but if he wasn't at least one of the targets, why did the man fire at the officer? After firing his first shot, time was of the essence for a quick, clean getaway without any witnesses."

"So when we're looking for the assailant, we need to consider why the police officer was shot. Besides guarding you, how does he tie to you and the judge?"

"He's had his share of arrests. Some of them could be tied to me since I would have prosecuted a lot of them. Officer Sims has been on the force for seven years and is exceptional."

"Then I know what I'll be doing. I need to add Officer Sims into the mix and review your case files again.

We'll concentrate on any that had all three of you involved. Did Sims ever arrest Mederos?"

"No. That doesn't mean he didn't bring in one of the gang members. A couple of them have gone to prison, and I seem to remember him on one of those cases about three or four years ago."

Uncle Ben headed for the hallway. "I'm going to bed. Unless you want me to take the first watch, Cade."

"No, I'm too wired. I don't know if my brain will shut down anytime soon." After his uncle left, Cade twisted toward Tory, his arm on the back cushion sliding down along her shoulders. "When you get up in the morning, you can help me with the case files, if you're up for it."

"I will be." She sighed. "I wanted Carlos to testify tomorrow, but I want his testimony to be over in a day's time. When you were talking to Paul outside my ER room, I made a call and delayed his transport until Friday. What if that was the reason for today? It would give Mederos another day to locate Carlos."

"I suppose that's possible. The best strategy would be to take Carlos out of the picture."

"My case hinges on his testimony. If he doesn't appear, I don't see getting a conviction."

Cade brushed a few strands of hair from her face, then traced her mouth with his forefinger. "You need your sleep. When this is over, we have to talk."

His feather light touch riveted her attention fully on him. "About what?"

"About how I can be in Michelle's life."

"You promised me you wouldn't say anything."

"And I won't. But after these past few days together,

I can't just walk away without being a part of her life in some way."

Anger, tamped down years ago, burst to life. "I won't let you disrupt her life, then move on when you feel like it."

He studied her a long moment. "Who said anything about moving on?"

"Tell me how many moves you've made since you left the army."

"This is my sixth one. Without family ties, it's easier for me than for others."

"So once you're tired of being around, it'll be easy for you to leave. There'll be another place that'll need you. That makes it convenient for someone who doesn't want to commit."

He pulled away, tension vibrating between them. "I committed to you once. I committed to my country, to protect the people of Texas. I don't have a problem doing that. Maybe you're really talking about yourself." He shot to his feet, his hands curled tight. "It didn't take you long to take the easy way out. It makes me question how committed you were to me fifteen years ago."

His words hurt, and yet they placed a seed of doubt in her mind. Had she sought the easy way out? She'd been afraid, confused and alone. Maybe he was right. But at the moment exhaustion had such a tight grip on her, she couldn't think clearly. She shouldn't have said what she had earlier—not with all Cade was doing for her and Michelle. This wasn't the time to mess with his focus on the job.

"Go to bed, Tory."

She struggled to her feet. Lightheaded, she swayed and nearly fell back onto the couch.

With lightning speed, Cade grasped her arm and steadied her. "C'mon. I'll walk with you. I need to go upstairs and check the windows anyway."

She wanted to tell him no, that she could go to her room by herself, but she couldn't muster the words. Her eyelids drooped, the medication she'd taken in the car finally kicking in. She allowed him to hold her close against his side.

By the time he opened her bedroom door, she couldn't even remember how she made it up the stairs. "Good night," she murmured and quickly disappeared inside.

She fell onto the bed completely dressed. What energy she had left siphoned from her body. Darkness swallowed her, and she gladly surrendered to it.

Cade stood at the dining room window, stretching and rolling his shoulders. He'd been sitting for hours, going through Tory's files and hadn't found any mention that she'd worked with Judge Parks and Officer Sims on a case, except one. A man destroyed his neighbor's car over a petty dispute. Then another time was charged with a third DUI and manslaughter. Nothing in those trials jumped out at him. The drunk driver was still in prison. Maybe he would find something later today when Tory had a chance to go through the cases. Maybe Sims was shot because he was guarding Tory and his presence had no other significance than that.

"Is something going on outside?" Uncle Ben asked.

"No." Cade turned from the window. "Just trying to figure out if something else is going on when we take Mederos out of the equation."

"It looks like you've been wrestling with that for a while." His uncle gestured toward Cade's head.

He raked his fingers through his hair, no doubt a mess after hitting one wall after another. "Yep. But after the evening I had, I was looking for a quick solution."

"What's really bothering you?"

"What makes you ask that?"

"I've known you for years. I can usually tell when something is eating at you."

"Do you…" He cleared his throat. "Do you think I have a commitment phobia?"

"When you do something, you do it one hundred percent. So no, I don't think that. What brought this on?" Uncle Ben held up his hand. "No need to tell me. Tory did."

"She thinks I didn't come back to El Rio because I felt she let me off the hook when she married Derek."

"When did she tell you that?"

"Tonight."

"After being in court all day, shot at, then going to the hospital. People say things they don't really mean when they're exhausted. But I have a feeling you believe her."

Cade nodded. "I wasn't in any shape to be a husband and father after my tour of duty. I know Derek kept things from Tory and pursued his own agenda where the baby was concerned, but he knew me well and he's the one I talked to after losing friends in combat."

"You were the only one who could decide if he did."

The sound of pounding footsteps rushing down the staircase drew Cade's attention.

Tory raced through the living room, her hair a wild

mess about her face, her complexion pale and her eyes wide with fear. "Is Michelle down here?"

"No, not that I know of." Cade moved toward her.

"She isn't upstairs. And her bed is empty."

"I've been in here for the past two hours. She didn't come downstairs in that time." His daughter would have had to hop over the bannister halfway down the steps for Cade to miss her.

"But she isn't anywhere upstairs."

"In order to leave, Michelle would have had to turn off the alarm system. I would have seen her. I'll go outside and check with the deputies and take a look around."

Tory spun toward the hallway. "I'm searching the first floor, then upstairs again."

"I'll help you," Uncle Ben said and joined her.

Cade grabbed a flashlight, punched the disarm code into the control pad, then went out the front door. The look on Tory's face made him question what he thought. She was convinced Michelle was gone. He didn't think so and prayed he was right.

After talking to the deputy sheriff posted out front, Cade started for the back of the house, examining all the windows as he went. There wasn't any reason for Michelle to leave. She was upset, but it was nighttime and it was ten miles to town. What happened to her mother had alarmed Michelle. He'd seen the fear in her expression.

When Cade rounded the rear of his house, more lights shone inside as Tory and his uncle searched it. At first he didn't see the second guard, but the man came around from the other side, spied him and quickened his pace toward Cade.

"Is something wrong?" the deputy asked.

"Michelle isn't in her room. I was checking the perimeter. Have you seen or heard anything unusual?"

"Other than the old mutt that hangs around the place, no. He was snooping a few bushes."

Cade kept moving, inspecting the next window. Something nagged him. Suddenly he retraced his steps and illuminated the roof of the porch where the window to Michelle's bedroom was. A dark movement caught his attention. He lifted his flashlight and shone it on his daughter, sitting where the porch met the house, her legs pulled up, her arms clasping them.

"Stay right there, Michelle." Cade hurried to the front door. Inside he found Tory and Uncle Ben coming from the kitchen. "I found her on the roof outside her bedroom window."

"What if she falls?" Tory raced for the staircase.

"It's pretty flat." Cade rushed after her.

Tory flipped on the overhead light and marched across the room and pulled the drapes open. "I didn't even think to check out here. Can she climb down to the ground?"

"Not without a ladder." He lowered his voice. "Let me talk to her first."

"Why?"

"I used to do the same thing when I was upset at Dad. Also I want to stress how important it is she follow directions so she doesn't fall."

Tory's mouth firmed into a frown. "She knows."

"And I think you need to keep some distance from this."

Her hands went to her waist. "What are you saying?"

"That you're too upset to talk to her."

For a long moment she didn't say anything, then her tense shoulders sagged. "You're right. We would only end up in a fight, and I don't have the energy for that."

"Go back to bed. If there's something you should know, I'll wake you."

After Tory walked across the hall and into her bedroom, Cade slid the window up and crawled through the opening. He couldn't see Michelle's face, but her drawn-up legs were visible from the light in her room. The air retained its warmth from earlier, but that wouldn't last long since the wind had kicked up.

"I used to come out here when I wanted to think." Cade sat near Tory, his eyes adjusting to the dark. He could make out her outline. He had no idea what she was thinking, although her body language shouted she was closed off.

Silence stretched from one minute to two.

Cade tried another approach. "Why are you out here?"

"Why are you?"

"To make sure you get back inside okay."

"I'm not gonna fall, if that's what you think."

"Good to know. But this is still not a good idea. I know you feel like no one can see you up here, but I did."

"Mom can leave the house. Why can't I?"

"Because she has to go to the trial. Personally I wish she didn't have to. It would be so much easier to keep her safe."

"I couldn't sleep. I just needed some fresh air. I'm…"

"What?"

"Frustrated. Wound up."

"And you need a way to release that."

"Yes, basketball does that for me. When I'm upset, I go shoot some hoops. Dad always understood that. Mom doesn't always. She doesn't like me being outside late at night, in our own driveway."

A casualty of Tory's job. And most likely as Michelle went through puberty, she would need to have a way to let off even more steam. "I had several ways to burn off frustration because there are days getting outside and running or playing basketball isn't doable. I haven't had time to string up my punching bag, but I will tomorrow."

"You box?"

"Not exactly. When I'm upset or frustrated, I imagine the bag is that problem. By the time I've finished punching it, I'm calmer and often have a solution to what's wrong. I was going to put it up in the bedroom you're sleeping in, so I will in the morning. It's good exercise. My gloves are too big for you, but I'll get a smaller pair for you to use."

"You don't have to do that. I won't be here that long."

"It's better than turning the living room into a basketball court."

Michelle giggled. "Okay. I'll give it a try, but I need this to be over. I heard my team lost today. I feel like I let them down."

Ah, so that was part of the reason Michelle's emotions fluctuated so much. "Remember there are other members of a team. When one player can't be there or do what's expected, they need to step up. The player who misses the last shot in a game that cost the team the win isn't the only one who's responsible for that loss. There were other times in the game other players could have stepped up and made a shot."

After a moment, she said, "I can see why you and Dad were friends. That's something he would tell me. Thanks for reminding me."

"He was a special guy." His throat constricted around the last word.

"Yes, and I miss him every…" Her voice faded into the silence.

"Day?"

She nodded.

"I miss him too," Cade said and meant every word. "We had some good times growing up." Cade heard Michelle yawn. "Maybe we should go back inside. I don't know about you, but I'm beat."

"Yeah, me too."

After Michelle crawled through the opened window, Cade followed then locked it. "This will end soon, I promise. Good night." He crossed to the door.

As he stepped into the hallway, Michelle said, "Thanks."

He looked at her and smiled. "Anytime."

The quiet sound of her closing the door made him hopeful he could have a relationship with his daughter—at least as a friend.

Before lunch, Tory dressed for court in a conservative dark gray suit, slid her feet into her comfortable slippers and crossed the hall to Michelle's bedroom, rapping softly. Cade had told her about his idea of hanging a punching bag for her.

In her workout clothes, Michelle opened her door. Behind her, a dark brown leather bag dangled from a stand while Michelle held protective gloves in her hands. Sweat glistened on her forehead.

"How do you like boxing?" Tory never thought she would ask her daughter that question.

Michelle grinned. "I feel good. Cade was right."

"I'm glad it's helping. Just wanted to see if you're okay."

"Are you going to work now? I thought court wouldn't convene until after lunch." Her daughter's gaze skimmed down Tory's body, and she laughed. "I know you don't like heels, but don't you think your slippers are too casual?"

"Funny. I could always start a new trend."

"You? I don't see you doing that."

Michelle's teasing tone lifted Tory's spirits. Was this Cade's doing? She grinned and started for the stairs. "You never know."

She followed the scent of coffee brewing and entered the kitchen as Cade set the pot on the counter after filling his mug. "Good morning."

He took a long look at her. "You sound upbeat. How's your arm?"

"The pain is manageable. I spoke to Michelle before coming downstairs. I think she really likes the punching bag."

"She's used to a lot of exercise. Being cooped up in this house these past few days has been hard on her. Coffee?"

"Yes, tons of it."

Cade poured it into a mug and passed it to Tory. "I've narrowed down the cases that might be tied to what's going on. Four look the most promising although there are more on my list. I thought we could discuss them before we go into town for the trial. I'll run down leads this afternoon. Paul called and wanted to know when we would arrive. He's staking out where you'll be entering to prevent what happened yesterday."

"How's Officer Sims?"

"He'll be fine. He's being guarded at the hospital. The San Antonio office sent another Texas Ranger to guard him."

With the one Texas Ranger protecting Judge Duggin, that made three on the case. "With Carlos Dietz's testimony on Monday, I'll be resting my case. Hopefully things will settle down after that."

"Maybe, especially if this is all tied to Mederos. But not all the cases on my list involving you, Judge Parks and/or Officer Sims are connected to Mederos. Where's Ben?"

"Here." The older man came into the kitchen from the dining room. "I was checking Cade's list for him. Do you want something to eat?"

"I'm starving."

"Breakfast or lunch since it's nearly eleven?" Ben walked to the refrigerator.

"Both. I skipped dinner last night."

"Let me see what I can come up with."

Before Tory left the room, she glanced back. "Whatever you fix will be good. By this time next week, I'm hoping to be out of your hair, and your life will be back to normal."

In the dining room, Tory sat diagonally from Cade. She wanted her life back. "I'm ready. Who is on the top of your list?"

He opened a file and slid it toward her. "Matthew Thorne. He was arrested for armed robbery."

"My first conviction as a prosecutor. I pushed for a

longer sentence. He got out of prison a couple of months ago on good behavior. Why him?"

"I can't find him. He didn't check in with his parole officer last month."

"I hadn't heard that."

"What can you tell me about him?"

"Mean and desperate. I shouldn't be surprised he went into hiding."

"And yet he got out of prison because of his good behavior."

"Because he can be like a chameleon." The time Matthew's behavior made a one-eighty turn in a blink of her eye sent goose bumps down her arms.

"Then there's Bobby Lindsey, arrested on drug charges. His prison time was extended because he beat up an inmate. If the guards hadn't stopped the fight, Bobby would have faced murder charges. He didn't become a member of Mederos's gang until he came out of prison two summers ago."

The memory of the bright sunny day outside the courtroom when Bobby blocked her path flooded her mind. "He threatened me in court when he was hauled away. I've seen him a few times in town. He actually came up to me and apologized for what he said before going away. But I didn't believe a word of it. The words were correct, but the look in his eyes shouted his hatred of me."

Cade nodded. "My third choice is Clarence Roberts. He died in prison two years ago. He was killed by an inmate."

"I didn't know that. He was convicted of rape. He kept insisting he was innocent, but the evidence said otherwise. The jury took less than three hours to come back with a guilty verdict."

"Roberts's and Lindsay's cases are the only ones that also included Officer Sims. Any of the other ones weren't serious with all three of you involved."

"I still think Mederos is behind all of this. I don't think Officer Sims was the intended victim yesterday."

Cade lowered his head and kneaded his nape. "That's a given possibility. I'm just looking at other options."

"Did you get any sleep last night?"

"Enough. I've gotten by on less before."

"That doesn't mean it's the best thing to do."

He frowned and looked at his list. "The last one was more recent. Manuel Freeman."

"He's still in prison and should be there for life for murder."

"But he told you he would kill you and he has several family members who have been vocal about the injustice he received at the hands of you and Judge Parks."

"True and any of them could be capable, especially his wife."

"Who is at the top of your list?" Cade set his piece of paper on the table.

"I've already told you. Mederos. He has the most to lose and lots of minions to do his dirty work."

"I learned the hard way that the easy, most obvious answer can get someone killed." He inhaled a breath, held it, then finally exhaled. "I was sure I had the right killer in a serial murder case when I first became a Texas Ranger. I was wrong and a married couple was murdered because I didn't consider all the options."

No one was infallible, but from the sound of his

voice, Cade expected it from himself. "We're human. We make mistakes."

"Mine cost two people their lives? I almost resigned, but Uncle Ben came all the way to Houston to give me a lecture."

"If not Mederos, then Matthew Thorne. He's gone underground. What's the reason?"

"I'm wondering the same. I've already contacted his parole officer in San Antonio this morning. The police are on alert for him, and he'll let me know if Thorne is found. After I drop you off in the courtroom, I'm looking for Bobby Lindsey. I want to have a few words with him. Also Pedro Mederos has been sighted in the area. If we can find him, maybe we can get to the bottom of Judge Parks's murder."

"You've been busy."

"Not just me but Sheriff Dawson, Chief Drake and Detective Alexander. Lieutenant Sanders has been co-ordinating from the police station, trying to get Paul to let him go into the field."

"That doesn't surprise me." Tory leaned toward Cade, clasping his arm. "Thank you. I hope by this time next week, everything is over with and the killer is in jail."

Cade took her hand and held it up between them. "So do I. I wish I could change the past, but I can't. I do know I want to be part of your life in the future."

"Don't you mean Michelle's?"

"Yes and no. Of course, her life, but you and I, we loved each other once. A lot has happened since then, but if we're at least friends, it would make it easier for me to be in Michelle's life. I'm not that twenty-year-old leaving to go to war. He died on the battlefield."

"And I'm not that innocent young girl who thought love could overcome anything. There's much more to a relationship than starry-eyed dreams."

Out of the corner of her eye she spied Ben coming into the dining room with a big grin on his face. "Breakfast/lunch is ready. I'll go upstairs and get Michelle while you two finish…discussing the case." He winked as he strolled past them.

"He's really enjoyed having Michelle here." Cade released her hand. "So do I."

"Even with all the emotional trauma she's brought with her?"

"I'd be worried if she didn't after all that's happened."

As Ben and Michelle came down the stairs, Tory stood. "Let's not talk about the case while we're eating."

"Sounds great after all the hours I put in on it."

Would that be enough? When this was over with, Tory had a lot to think about—her job, her relationship with Michelle…and Cade. The only things she knew right now were that she would protect her daughter at all costs and herself from being hurt again as Cade had done fifteen years ago.

Later that evening, Cade brought Tory a mug in the living room. "Decaf. I thought we both could use a good night's sleep after the past couple of days. How's the prep for the star witness going?"

"I talked with the US Marshals guarding him. They're bringing him to the courthouse an hour early on Monday so I can go through what Carlos should expect from Mederos's attorney. Once Carlos went into hiding, I haven't had any contact with him, but the marshal in charge assures me that he's ready to testify. I'm ready too."

Cade sat next to her on the couch. "Me too. I thought I had a lead on Pedro this afternoon. When I got there, I found evidence someone had been hiding out in the cabin, but whoever had was gone. What concerned me was that there was evidence of a fight. I processed the scene, and the few latent prints I found were Pedro's."

"Why didn't you tell me this earlier?" She twisted toward him.

"Because you fell asleep on the ride to the ranch from the courthouse." He brushed his finger across her cheek. "This trial has taken a toll not only on Michelle but you too."

"Let's hope it'll be quiet for the weekend. Thank goodness everything was routine today at the courthouse after yesterday."

"With every police officer in the area there, it would have been hard for Mederos to stage something."

"But not impossible. Now we only have to get through Monday."

Cade wanted to keep her near. After she'd been grazed with a bullet the day before, he realized how close he'd come to losing her for good. He'd promised to keep her and Michelle safe, and he would. Somehow. "Another piece of news. Matthew Thorne was picked up in Austin, drunk. He's in jail for jumping parole."

"Do you know why he did?"

"No, but his parole officer will talk with him tomorrow and let me know what Thorne says."

"Did anything else happen today while I was in court?" Tory tried to stifle a yawn but couldn't.

"Nope. I wish I could tell you I discovered the person behind what's been going on."

"At least Michelle is better. Ben told me she didn't give him any grief about doing her schoolwork."

"How does she do in school?" He wanted to know everything. All he had were photos of her as a child or an occasional tidbit that Uncle Ben had heard.

"You mean you don't know that?"

He shook his head. "It isn't something the school would release to me."

"She's made As and Bs. Loves math and science. Hates history. English is okay. Does that sound like someone you know?"

"Can a love of a subject be hereditary?"

Tory shrugged. "Half her genes are yours."

Pride swelled in his chest. He was part of Michelle. He'd never really thought of it that way. "I missed a lot." Regret coated each word.

"Yes. But if you want—" she covered another yawn "—you can be a friend in her life."

"But not her father?" slipped out before he could censor his thoughts.

Tory stiffened. "I have to think about what's best for Michelle. I won't shatter her love for Derek. He was a good father." She set her mug on the end table by her and rose. "It's time I turn in. This week has caught up with me."

He started to stand, but she waved him off.

"Cade, we'll talk tomorrow."

He'd known the second he'd asked that question about being Michelle's father that it had been the wrong time. Unfortunately, there never seemed to be a right time. He leaned his head on the back cushion and stared at the ceiling. Had he just blown it?

He decided to go through the house and check the windows and doors, then devote the next few hours to going back through the trial files that were the most promising—again. He hoped the perpetrator turned out to be Thorne and that he remained in jail.

But the only new thing he'd found two hours later was that Clarence Roberts had been rumored to be trying to become a member of Mederos's gang. Was he when he was convicted? So two of the four files he'd singled out had a connection to Mederos. The man did have his fingers into everything in the county—unless Tory managed to convince the jury he was guilty.

Someone pounded on the front door. "Open up." It sounded like one of the guards outside.

Cade hurried to the entrance, checked to make sure it was the deputy sheriff, then pulled the door open. "What's wrong?"

"Fire," the deputy said, pointing toward the barn.

Cade stepped outside, the brisk wind whipping his clothes. A blaze lit the sky.

SEVEN

A hand shook Tory's arm. She wanted to keep sleeping and tried to roll away.

"Get up, Tory. Now." Urgency in Cade's voice jerked her awake.

She blinked repeatedly as her eyes adjusted to the bright light that flooded her bedroom. Cade stood over her, his face sober. He flicked his gaze toward the window.

"The barn's on fire and it's windy, spreading the flames all around. We don't have much time to get out of here. Wake up Michelle and both of you pack what you need for a few days."

She sat straight up, trying to digest what he was telling her. "Has the fire department been called?"

"Yes, one of the deputies did."

"We should try to help put it out."

Cade strode to the window facing in that direction and shoved the drapes back. The yellow-orange glow of the barn filled her view, obscuring the dark sky. She scurried from the bed and went to the window as Cade headed for the hallway.

"Meet me in the garage in five minutes."

For a few seconds, the sparks caught on the wind and swirled about, reminding her of summer nights as a kid trying to catch the fireflies. One ember landed about twenty yards from the house. The grass caught fire in seconds.

She whirled around and darted across the hall into Michelle's room. She pulled on her daughter's arm. "Get up. The barn is burning. We have to leave. Pack what you can in three minutes."

"What about Bella?" As Michelle said the pregnant dog's name, Bella lifted her head from the pillow where she slept on the floor.

"Get her leash and lead her out. The fire might scare her. You may have to carry her in the end."

Tory hurried back to her room and began flinging everything she owned into a duffel bag. She glanced at the window, wishing the fire wasn't spreading so quickly, but not surprised because the area was suffering through a drought. When she finished, she grabbed her overnight piece of luggage along with the filled one and scrambled down the stairs to stuff the files into the empty suitcase.

As she cleared the dining room table, Cade helped her. Ben came down the stairs holding Bella while Michelle carried the bags.

"Put everything in the car in the garage," Cade said to his uncle and Michelle.

"Where are the deputies?" Ben asked as he passed the dining room table, the sound of sirens in the distance.

"They're hosing down the roof. The barn is gone and the fire is turning into a wildfire." Cade put the last court file into the suitcase, then closed it. "Let's go."

"What about your house, the ranch?" Cade had grown up here, and Tory's presence had put him and the ranch in danger.

"We can't do anything else. I just hope the firefighters can stop this from spreading too much. The horses are in the pastures in the opposite direction of the wind. And one of the deputies said he saw Buddy and the cats running from the barn, so they're safe too."

"Where will we go?" Tory followed Cade through the kitchen.

"I have an idea, but I have to make a few calls. This time no one will know where we are but us."

While Cade stowed the bags in the rear compartment of the SUV, Tory climbed into the front passenger seat. Ben, Michelle and Bella were in the back. Cade didn't punch the garage door opener until he sat behind the steering wheel. Tory glanced at the clock. One in the morning.

When Cade pulled out, he stopped and assessed their surroundings. Small fires littered the landscape, the scent of smoke heavy. Tory stared at the road that led to the highway. On both sides of it, the grass had caught fire. In spite of what the two deputies had done, an ember landed on the garage roof and burst into flames.

"How do we get out of here?" Tory asked as she spied the flashing lights of the fire engines.

"Stay in here. I'll be back in a second." Cade got out of his SUV and rushed to the deputy sheriff's car behind him.

Everywhere Tory looked, flames rapidly devoured the dry terrain and kept creeping closer to them. When the fire engines halted on the highway, she knew they were in trouble. If the fire department wasn't going to risk going down the dirt road, then how could they leave the ranch that way? She tried to think what the terrain on the south side of the house was like. Rocky. Crevices in places.

When Cade returned, he shifted toward them. "We're going to go out using the dirt road. The deputies will go first. We'll follow. The fire is jumping the road, but because there's no vegetation the road itself should be okay. All windows closed. I'm closing the vents. Uncle Ben, get the wool blankets in the back and give each of us one. If we have to stop on the road, cover yourself with a blanket and get on the floor."

Tory noted the limited room for the driver with the steering wheel. "How about you?"

"I'll be fine. I'm hoping we can drive out without a problem. The fire department will be operating from the highway and try to contain the wildfire, but it's been pretty dry lately. The sheriff is closing the highway." Cade put the car into Drive and trailed behind the deputy's SUV.

Tory glanced at Michelle. "Okay?"

Her daughter nodded, her eyes huge.

"I'll watch out the left side. Tory, you watch out the right," Ben said. "We'll be all right. I put our emergency supply kit in the back. We've done all we can do for now."

As Cade moved forward, smoke swallowed the deputy's patrol vehicle in front. Cade was essentially driving blind with only a foot visibility. Tory's heartbeat accelerated as he slowed the SUV in order to prepare for the unexpected. Sweat beaded her forehead and ran into her eyes, stinging them. Or was it the smoke she could smell in spite of closing the windows and vents?

Please, Lord, help us get to safety.

Through the gray density surrounding the car, Tory glimpsed the flashing red lights. The drive was only a half a mile from the highway, but to Tory it seemed an eternity when Cade turned onto the asphalt road, situated on a rise about ten feet above the ranch.

A firefighter approached the driver side of the SUV.

Cade cracked the window and asked, "Which is the best way out of here?"

"South, for the time being."

Cade poked a business card out of the small opening. "This is my contact number. If you can't get hold of me, call Police Chief Paul Drake. He'll know how."

"Will do." The man stepped back.

As they drove away from the inferno raging across Cade's land, Ben passed out bottles of water.

The cool liquid helped soothe the dryness in Tory's throat. "Where are we going?"

"When we are away and I don't think anyone is following us, I'll make a call. I have a place in mind."

Tory lowered her voice, saying, "Just us?"

"If this has something to do with Mederos, he'll need to make his move this weekend."

"Why? A member of my office can handle the questioning of the star witness on Monday."

"I'm sure you think someone else could do the case you've been living the past couple of months, but you need to be there." Cade threw a glance over his shoulder then whispered, "We'll talk later." He nodded his head toward Michelle.

"I understand." Obviously he didn't want to talk in front of Michelle. She would have to wait. His tone indicated even Mederos's verdict wouldn't take away the threat to her and her daughter. Would this ever end?

"Is Michelle all right?" Cade asked when Tory came into the main room of the rustic cabin, used once as a safe house.

"As well as can be expected. The fire scared her. How fast it spread. How close it came to your house. She was worried about your home burning too."

"I called Paul on the landline here, and he said the fire department is still fighting the grass fire. The barn is gone, but a section over the garage is the only part damaged at the house. So far, they've managed to keep the blaze away from my home. If the wind doesn't change it should be fixable."

"She gave me this reluctantly." Tory handed him Michelle's cell phone, then eased down onto the couch near Cade.

"I've disabled all cell phones. They can't be used here. We don't want whoever set the barn on fire finding us. No one knows where we are. I was careful driving away. We should be all right this weekend. I need to leave to get some supplies, but there's a store about a mile from here. Other than that, I'm staying here and working the case. Paul will run down anything I need. Did you call the US Marshals on the landline about the new number to call if needed?"

"Yes, everything is still going well there. Carlos is eager to get this over with. So am I."

He smiled. "We all feel that way."

"When this is over, I'm going to make a batch of cookies for the two deputies guarding us. If they hadn't been there tonight, we might not have had time to get to safety."

"I want to buy them a thick, juicy steak. My house is still standing because they watered it down. That and God was looking out for us tonight."

Tory leaned her head against the back cushion, her eyelids heavy.

"Go to bed."

"I could say the same for you. I'm waiting for Michelle to fall asleep."

"I'm waiting for Uncle Ben to get a little more rest. Good thing we're taking shifts at night. He snores."

"Michelle is all over the place when she sleeps. Once I found her on the floor sleeping in the doorway when she was four."

Cade loved hearing about Michelle as a child, but each story left an emptiness in him. He'd made a mistake thinking he could come home and be part of his daughter's life from afar. That it would satisfy a need he had, fill a loneliness. Instead, being around her only made it worse.

"When did she start playing basketball?"

"As soon as she could hold the ball. Derek put the hoop down to a level she could handle."

Cade really couldn't blame Derek about keeping certain information from Tory concerning what had really happened. Cade had never pushed to talk with her directly. He'd known he couldn't handle a renewed relationship with her on top of everything else he was going through. "I wish I could have seen that."

"I have a video of her at the age of six."

"Did you take a lot of videos of Michelle?"

"Either I did or Derek."

"Maybe one day I could see them."

Bending toward him, Tory placed her hand on his forearm. "Sure."

He leaned forward, only a few inches from her. When she slid her eyes closed, he cradled her face and kissed her. He'd missed her more than he ever realized. He'd thought he was all right living alone. Now he was having misgivings. He drew her to him, his arms encircling her while he deepened the kiss.

A sound invaded his mind. He pulled back a few inches and glanced over her shoulder. "Uncle Ben," he whispered to Tory.

His uncle grinned. "Maybe I should go back to bed."

"No. If I'm going to figure out what's going on here, I need to rest." Cade released his hold on Tory and already missed her touch.

"Me too. I'm sure Michelle is asleep by now." Tory pushed off the couch. "Good night, Cade, Ben."

When Tory left the room, his uncle assessed Cade. "Hmm. Are you two mending fences?"

"No—yes."

Uncle Ben laughed. "Well, which is it?"

"I can't answer for Tory, but all I want to do is put the past behind us. It's not important anymore. It wasn't my fault, and it wasn't her fault we weren't together."

His uncle peered at the two mugs. "Is there any coffee left?"

"Yes, but it's decaf."

"That's worthless. Coffee is meant to have caffeine."

Cade picked up the cups and started for the kitchen. "See you in a few hours."

When he walked down the short hall, he paused at Tory's door. He needed to shove down all the reemerging emotions concerning Tory. His first and only priority was keeping her and Michelle alive.

"I won! I won!" Michelle pumped her arm in the air.

"She's never learned to win gracefully," Tory said with a chuckle as the four of them sat at the kitchen table in the cabin late Sunday morning, playing cribbage.

"What's the point of playing if you aren't gonna try and win?" Her daughter pulled the rubber band from her ponytail and shook her hair free. "Can we go for a walk since we're at a secret location? Bella needs to get outside. She told me today. Pretty please." Michelle rubbed the dog behind her ears.

"Yes, I'd like to stretch my legs," Tory said, staring out the window at the thick woods surrounding the place about two hundred yards off the highway. Unless someone had followed them here, which Cade had made sure hadn't happened, they would be safe. She was beginning to understand what Michelle had been going through the past week.

"No." Cade boxed up the board game. "Not a good idea."

"Why? *I* don't even know where we are." Michelle set her elbow on the table and rested her chin in her cupped hand.

"And that's the way I want it to stay." Cade rose and went to the coffeepot and refilled his mug.

"That's not fair. You left yesterday." Michelle flounced to the refrigerator and took a soft drink out. "I don't have a punching bag here to use. I can't talk to my friends. I'm bored."

"You're enjoying that—" Cade pointed at the can her daughter held "—because I did go get some food to eat. And believe me I went out of my way not to be recognized."

Even to the point of using an old truck parked in the detached garage behind the cabin rather than the SUV. "Michelle, this should be over soon. Be patient."

Ben stood. "I can put you through a series of exercises that will leave you exhausted. How about it? I'm over sixty years old, but I'll be able to outlast you."

"No way, old man." A grin teased her daughter's mouth.

"You're on, girlie."

When the two left the kitchen with Bella following, Tory raised her empty mug. "I'd like a refill."

Cade brought the pot to the table and poured coffee into her cup.

"It looks like Ben has figured out Michelle."

"So I need to challenge her."

"She's very competitive. She got that from her father."

"Which one?"

"Both," she mouthed.

Cade chuckled. "Yep, you're right, and I should have known that."

"I really wish we could go for a walk."

"I know. Sitting around waiting for something to happen isn't fun." Cade placed his chair kitty-corner with hers. "I thought we were gonna have another teenage moment."

"Oh, don't think it won't happen. Michelle's mood can change like this." Tory snapped her fingers. "I wasn't like that when I was her age."

Cade looked down at the table, avoiding Tory's eyes. "What?"

"Remember that time you stormed out of the dance because I was dancing with your best friend, and you're the one who suggested it?"

"A fast dance, not a slow one."

"Oh, you should have clarified that."

"I'll remember the next time we're at a dance."

"Our circumstances are much different now. We aren't a couple."

"Thanks for pointing out the obvious." She walked to the sink and put her mug in it. Why had what he'd said upset her?

He came up behind her and clasped her arms, then whispered into her ear, "Do you want that to change?"

Did she? Could she expose herself to being hurt by him again? She realized in that moment she'd never had to worry about her heart being torn apart while married to Derek because she hadn't felt the same way about him as she had for Cade. Her love for Derek was a different kind of love—maybe a better one. Or rather, safer one.

Tory swept around to face Cade, her back pressed against the counter. He was too near, and yet his very presence comforted her. So many mixed feelings bombarded her. "The only thing I can focus on right now is staying alive and keeping Michelle safe physically and emotionally."

"I want the same thing. She's my daughter too," he said in a low voice.

A gasp behind Cade sent a shaft of fear rushing through Tory. She and Cade turned around.

There stood Michelle.

EIGHT

The stunned look and pale cast to his daughter's skin accompanied by a blank stare quickly evolved into anger. Michelle glared at Cade. "I am not your daughter." She raced from the kitchen.

Uncle Ben's yell to stop propelled Tory and Cade into action. The front door slammed closed. Cade made it to the exit first, his hand on the knob.

Tory grabbed Cade's arm. "I'm going after her."

"No, you aren't."

"I'm her mother." She tried to wedge herself between him and the door.

He planted his body in her way, his arms crossed. "You're the one who has someone after her. It's too dangerous."

Uncle Ben approached. "Both of you. Get out of the way. What happened?"

"Michelle overheard Cade say he was her father."

His uncle whistled. "Neither one of you should go after her. I will. Step away from the door."

Cade realized his uncle was right. His and Tory's presence would only cause her to flee faster. He moved away while Tory stared at Uncle Ben a few more seconds before doing the same.

Immediately after his uncle left the cabin, he moved to the living room window to watch.

Tory came up beside him. "You shouldn't have said that."

"I didn't know she was behind me and had such good hearing. I'm sorry this happened."

"I don't think you are. You want her to know you're her father."

"Not if she's going to flip out."

"You just changed everything she thought was true."

"No, I didn't. You're the one who let everyone think Derek was Michelle's father. Her whole life has been based on a lie you condoned fifteen years ago because you were afraid of what people would say and think." Locked away for so long, the words spilled out of him. He'd thought he'd dealt with those feelings and accepted what had happened.

But he'd been wrong.

Tears glistened in her eyes. She glared at him, much like Michelle had.

"I shouldn't have said that," he murmured, realizing it was too late for them. He'd made a big mistake coming home.

Tory spun toward the window, keeping her gaze trained on the landscape out front.

Cade strode to the door and opened it to watch from the entrance. He needed space. He needed this case over.

Out of the corner of his eye, he spied Uncle Ben with his arm around Michelle walking toward the cabin. *Thank You, Lord. Any suggestions how I handle this mess?*

Cade sidestepped to allow the two of them inside. Michelle kept her head down, her shoulders hunched. As he closed the door, she shrugged away from Uncle Ben and stormed toward her bedroom.

"Michelle." Tory took several paces toward her daughter. "Let me explain."

Michelle halted, her arms ramrod straight at her sides. Her back to them, she said, "There is nothing to explain. You lied to me for fourteen years." She charged into the corridor, disappearing. A door slammed shut so loudly a nearby picture shook on the wall.

Tory didn't say anything for a long moment, then she faced Uncle Ben. "What did she say?"

"She asked me if it was true, and I told her yes."

"Anything else?"

"No, she just listened to me tell her she needed to talk to both of you. When I told her she wasn't safe outside the cabin and we needed to go back inside, she followed me without a word. She didn't yell, cry—anything."

"Thanks, Ben, for going to get her. You're right. She would have run from me." Tory's shoulders sagged like Michelle's as though she'd been defeated.

"I'm going into the kitchen to fix us something for lunch. You two need to talk." Uncle Ben hurried out of the room.

Cade wanted to be in Michelle's life but not like this. He would take that remark back in an instant, if he could. "Is there anything I can do?"

"You've done enough. I created this problem, and I need to deal with it—alone." Tory started for her bedroom she shared with Michelle, stopped and changed her direction. She followed Uncle Ben into the kitchen.

The least he could do was give Tory space. This would be a good time to go outside and walk the perimeter. He knew there was no such thing as a 100 percent safe house. Outside in the clearing, he took a deep breath of the fresh air, relishing the scent of earth and pine trees. The sun beamed as though God was smiling down upon him. All he could hope was that Michelle and Tory would talk to him before this assignment was over. Not dealing with the problem wouldn't make it go away. He'd learned that when he'd tried to ignore his emotional well-being after returning to the States from the Middle East.

He needed to put himself into Michelle's shoes and understand the pain his words had caused. He'd ripped the fabric of what she'd thought was true into two pieces. Helplessness blanketed him and smothered any hope he'd had of being in his daughter's life.

As he circled the cabin, his attention focused on his surroundings, he noted anywhere someone could hide and watch the place. Only a few but even one was too many.

Tory seemed to think with the testimony of Carlos Dietz tomorrow, the danger would be over. And she might be right, especially if Mederos was after her because she knew where Carlos was being kept. But until they caught the person behind the incidents, he couldn't rest.

Later that evening Ben entered the kitchen with the tray of food he took Michelle for dinner. Tory sat at one end of the table while Cade was at the other. She glanced up from her notes of what she would ask Carlos tomorrow.

Ben took a seat between them. "I've given up our room to Michelle, Cade. When we aren't on guard tonight, we can sleep on the couch in the living room."

Tory put her pad down. "No, I can't let you do that. This has gone on long enough. You both need your rest."

"I'll be fine," Cade murmured, then returned to a file he was going through.

Ben raked his hand through his thinning hair. "Tory, you haven't asked my opinion about this situation, but I'm gonna give it to you anyway. Give Michelle the space she needs to calm down. Most of her anger is directed at you. She still hopes this could be a mistake."

Her nerves shredded, Tory gritted her teeth. This situation couldn't get any worse. "Well, it isn't. She'll have to learn to accept it." Her stomach knotted in a jumble of conflicting emotions from helplessness to frustration to fury. If there was such a thing as do-overs, she wouldn't have made the choices she had. Her father hadn't been well and the news she was going to have a baby out of wedlock would have crushed him. Ben was probably right, but she hated going into court tomorrow with this looming between her and Michelle. She needed to focus on the trial. She needed to nail the questioning of the star witness or this would all be for nothing.

Tory shoved her chair back and bolted to her feet. "I'll be in the living room until you want to go to sleep, Ben."

She drilled her glare into the top of Cade's head, still bent over a file. His uncle nodded at her. She left the room and settled on the couch, her legal pad in her lap. But the words melded all together. And when she finally read her list of points to make, they blended into one big tangle in her mind. Like her life.

She looked at her hands. They were shaking. She fisted them, but that didn't stop their trembling. Her well-ordered life was falling apart around her. When she first heard Cade was returning to El Rio to take over Ranger Eastman's duties, in her gut she'd known something like this was a possibility. That was why she had kept her distance from him for his first three weeks although she had consulted with the previous Texas Ranger a couple of times a month.

When Derek had asked her to marry him and let him be the father of her child, she'd thought her problems were over. But in reality they had only begun.

Lord, please forgive me for what I did fifteen years ago. Living a lie wasn't the best idea for any of them. Now she had to face the consequences of her bad decisions and actions.

"Cade, get up."

The urgent words dragged Cade from a much-needed sleep. He popped one eyelid open to find Uncle Ben bending over him.

"Michelle's missing."

"Again?"

"She's not in the cabin, and the alarm system has been turned off."

Cade shot up on the couch. "What time is it?"

"Six." His uncle straightened. "I even peeked into Tory's room, hoping Michelle went to see her mom. She didn't."

"Is Tory up?" Cade swung his legs off the sofa, using the time to clear the sleep from the corners of his mind.

He had to focus on the problem at hand. "I'll go outside and look around. I wouldn't put it past her to get some fresh air now while it's still semi-dark."

"I hope so. I could see Michelle thinking the dark would conceal her from the bad guys."

Cade put on his boots. "How did you find out Michelle was gone?"

"When I was in the hallway, I noticed the door to that bedroom was ajar. It wasn't the last time I walked through the cabin. I wasn't too worried until I saw the alarm system was off. She was mighty angry last night. I think she left of her own free will, but even if she did, she's in danger."

Tory rushed into the living room, wearing the same clothes as yesterday. "We've got to find her before someone else does. Did you check to see if she took her cell phone? Knowing my daughter, she'd probably call Emma or Jodie. When she's upset, she can be on the phone for hours talking or texting."

Cade rose and went to a drawer in the cabinet. "She didn't take it. I have the batteries in a different place. It does look like someone has been in the drawer. They aren't in the same arrangement I had them." He grabbed his jacket and headed for the only door into the house. "Tory, call her friends on the landline. See if she's contacted them."

When he stepped outside, Cade panned the area, trying to determine which way she might have gone. They were five miles from El Rio, but there were a mini-mart and diner less than a mile from the cabin. Or was she out in the woods somewhere? If she came into the living room and risked him waking up to get her phone, then that most likely meant she wanted to talk to her friends.

Tory opened the front door and stuck her head out. "She called Emma all upset about forty minutes ago. Emma was asleep so it went to voice mail."

"Did you get the number where she called from?"

"Yes." Tory recited the number. "I'm not familiar with that one."

"Call Paul and have him trace it. I'm scouting around the cabin and a little into the woods."

"I'll help."

"No. You need to get ready for the trial. I'll find our daughter. Lock this door."

Cade spent the next twenty minutes checking the cabin's surroundings. With each moment that passed, his gut tightened until it was a rock weighing him down. It was difficult enough to protect a person, but when she didn't want it, it made the job triple hard.

Please, Lord. Help me find my daughter.

He hoped the trial and need to be with Tory and Michelle ended today with the testimony of Carlos Dietz. But he had a feeling deep down there was more to what was going on. Without concrete proof they were safe, he couldn't walk away. He wasn't even sure he could when they were out of danger. But Michelle's action clearly indicated she wanted nothing to do with him.

I'll cross that bridge when I have to.

Cade returned to the cabin and pounded on the door.

Uncle Ben answered. "She was at the mini-mart near here. I tried calling the number. No one answered."

"I'm taking the pickup and will bring her home. If I'm not back in half an hour, have Tory call Paul and the judge."

Tory peeked around his uncle. "I'm coming with you."

"No."

"We've already come this far. Stay here with my uncle. Get ready to go to the courthouse."

"Then call as soon as you find her. If you aren't taking yours, borrow someone's phone."

"Do you have a recent picture of her?" Cade asked.

After Tory retrieved a photo from her purse, Cade strode to the truck, slipped inside, then drove to the store where he prayed Michelle still was. When he walked inside, he scanned the mini-mart. Only the clerk and two customers—a woman, dressed for work in an office, and a young man in jeans, boots and a leather jacket. No sign of Michelle.

As Cade made his way to the counter to show the clerk her photo, another man entered. His scruffy appearance coupled with a matted, long black beard put Cade on alert. He'd seen him somewhere recently. Was it when he interviewed Mederos's gang? Had he been in the background? He couldn't shake the feeling something was off.

Cade showed the clerk Michelle's photo. "Have you seen her in here today?"

"Yeah, she went into there a while back." The young man jerked his thumb to the left.

"Thanks." As he kept his eye on the customers, Cade strolled to the diner entrance and pushed through the doorway into the restaurant.

The scruffy middle-aged man followed Cade into the restaurant. The hairs on his nape tingled. Cade moved to the side to let him pass him while searching the crowded eatery. He kept his attention on both the room full of people and the bearded guy, who paused a few feet away and swept his gaze over the throng.

Cade couldn't see everyone. The counter was in the way of a section of the big room. He moved forward to survey the rest of the place.

The big bearded man blocked his path. "Can you lend me some money for food?"

The odor emitting from the guy nauseated Cade, who looked into his bleak expression. He remembered where he'd seen him. Loitering in the park across from the courthouse. He could be one of the homeless people who hung out at the park or a person planted there by Mederos to keep an eye out. With his wallet back at the cabin, Cade dug into his pocket and withdrew a couple of dollars in change.

"That's all I have," Cade said, then started to skirt the man.

He grabbed Cade's arm, halting him. He prepared to defend himself when the man grinned, two of his teeth missing, and said, "Thanks, mister."

Cade nodded and pulled his arm out of the guy's grasp. A movement drew his attention across the room. All he caught sight of was a tall person with a gray hoodie on disappearing down the hallway that led to the restrooms. Michelle had a gray hoodie.

He weaved his way through tables as quickly as he could. As he rounded the counter, the door to the women's bathroom clicked shut. He closed the distance and knocked. No one said anything.

He put his hand on the knob. "This is Ranger Morgan. I'm coming into the restroom." When he tried to open the door, it was locked. He returned to the main room and found the couple who owned the diner.

"Do you have a key to unlock the ladies' bathroom?" Cade showed them his badge.

The wife scurried to the cash register and removed something from it. "This will work—" she put the key in Cade's hand "—ever since a little girl locked herself inside and wouldn't open the door."

"Did you see the thin person in a gray hoodie?"

"No. It's been a busy morning. Amber waited on the hoodie guy or gal." The wife of the owner signaled a short redhead. "Ask Amber." Then she left to return to the cash register.

Cade showed the redheaded waitress the photo. "Was this the person in a hoodie that you served?"

"I was about ready to tell her to leave. She ordered a Coke and was taking her sweet time drinking it. Soon this place will be so busy we'll need her table."

"How long has she been here?"

"About forty-five minutes."

"Thanks."

When Cade unlocked the door and stepped into the empty restroom, his focus centered on the open window. He stuck his head outside it and heard an engine revving. He raced from the bathroom, through the diner and out the front door. A car and someone dressed in black on a motorcycle were speeding away. He searched the area. Was Michelle with them? There was something familiar about the biker.

Cade rushed for his truck, hopped in and pulled out of the parking lot. With no phone, he had no way of calling for backup, but he had to keep his eye on the car and motorcycle. He couldn't shake the feeling Michelle was in the vehicle or the trunk. At least he had his gun, but he needed to call Paul and the sheriff.

Then he remembered the throwaway cell kept in the glove compartment, put there for situations just like this one. As he pressed his foot on the accelerator, he leaned over and retrieved the phone. He called 911 and asked to be put through to the police chief.

When the car and bike turned onto another small county road, Paul came on the line. Cade told him where he was going. "I don't know for sure Michelle is with them, but I think so. In case I'm wrong, send an officer to the diner connected to the mini-mart at the intersection of the highway and County Road 5476."

"I'll get a roadblock set up. I'll call Sheriff Dawson."

After hanging up with the police chief, Cade made another call to the cabin. His uncle answered.

Cade explained what happened at the diner.

"I'll check around in case Michelle isn't in the car you're following. She could be hiding and might come out if she sees me."

"Yeah, she's not angry at you like she is with Tory and me."

Cade disconnected and tossed the phone on the passenger seat within reach, then returned his full attention to the pair of vehicles about a hundred yards ahead of him. He tamped down his anxiety and prayed he'd made the right call. The way the two ahead of him left the diner indicated something wasn't quite right.

When the car and motorcycle increased their speed, Cade did too but kept some distance between them until the roadblock was in place. If Michelle was in the car, he had to keep her safe.

Up ahead two deputy sheriffs' vehicles were parked across the road. The car slowed while the bike made a U-turn and headed toward Cade. He slammed on the brakes, jumped from the cab and drew his gun.

"Stop. Now," he shouted over the noise of the motorcycle.

The biker skidded to a stop, gripping the handlebars.

"Keep your hands there." Cade stepped from behind his open pickup door and walked toward the man. He remembered he'd seen him with some of Mederos's gang when he was questioning them about Pedro.

"I ain't done nuthin' wrong."

"Then why are you avoiding a roadblock?"

Suddenly the biker revved his engine as though he meant to take off.

"What if Michelle is here somewhere?" Tory asked Ben as he pulled into the parking lot at the diner.

"Cade said that was a possibility, but with us and the police at the diner we should be able to find her."

"But if my daughter is in the car, that means she's been kidnapped and…"

Ben frowned. "Let's think positive. We'll get her back, and she'll be fine."

"You and I know what can happen. We've seen kidnappings go wrong before."

"That's what's so hard about the work we do. It's hard to stay positive." Ben grasped the handle. "Paul's here. I'm going to see what they're doing about searching around the truck stop."

"I'm coming with you."

"Don't. Remember the sniper. He already got a piece of you once."

"I need to talk to Paul about the witness transfer."

"I'll have him come over and see you." When Ben left, the sound of the door shutting emphasized how little freedom she had because of the Mederos trial.

The confined feeling made her want even more a guilty verdict. Criminals shouldn't be able to get away with intimidating others like Mederos had for years.

When Ben returned, Paul accompanied him and climbed into the backseat. "Ben said you wanted to talk to me."

"I need to use a cell phone to call Judge Duggin and then the US Marshals if this can't be resolved in the next hour. I can't leave until Michelle is found. I'm hoping for a delay in the trial. I promised Carlos I would be there when he testifies."

"I don't have enough manpower to support the protection of your witness *and* searching for Michelle. I know my officers won't be the only ones guarding the witness, but everyone we can put in place keeps him safer. The sheriff will let me know what happens at the roadblock." Paul removed a cell phone from his pocket. "This is my personal one. Use it."

"What roadblock?"

"The sheriff had a couple of deputies set one up on County Road 5476. That's where the car and motorcycle were heading. The last I heard the biker had made a run for it."

So many people put at risk because of what was happening. "You think Michelle is in the car."

"Possibly. My men are scouring this area and haven't found her. A couple of people inside confirmed she was here. We'll find her, Tory." Paul patted her shoulder then left the SUV.

"I'd always thought Michelle and I had a good relationship. But in a short time, that bond has been destroyed. I made a mistake how I handled the whole situation fifteen years ago. Now I don't know if my daughter will ever forgive me." And she didn't know if she would forgive herself, especially if anything happened to another innocent person.

Ben twisted toward her. "You aren't angry that she left the cabin when she shouldn't have?"

"Of course, I am. I tried talking to her, but she wasn't hearing me. Honesty has always been important to me. She'll never believe me again." Tory dropped her head.

"Look at me." Ben took her hand and waited until she glanced up. "At worst, you made a mistake. There isn't a soul on earth who hasn't. I'm not saying it will be easy, but if y'all have a good foundation, she'll understand the whys. Give her time."

What if I don't have that time? Tears swelled into her eyes. "I need to do something…" She yanked her hand from his grasp. "I can't sit here any longer just waiting." She gripped the handle and started opening the door.

"Wait. Paul Drake is coming this way. See what he has to say before you get out and expose yourself."

Cade braced himself for an attempted escape. "Turn the motorcycle off, or I'll shoot your tires. You aren't going anywhere."

The biker glared at him, probably trying to gauge if he spoke the truth.

"I never make threats that I won't back up." Cade stepped away from the truck and sauntered toward the man as though he was deadly calm and capable of moving fast enough to stop the guy from leaving the roadblock.

The burly man revved the engine one more time then switched it off.

"Move away from the bike." As he approached the

motorcyclist, Cade kept his weapon aimed at him. He wouldn't put it past the guy to still try something. "Put your hands behind your back and turn around."

When the biker complied, Cade clapped handcuffs around his wrists. Then he pushed him forward toward the deputies and the stopped car. As he neared the roadblock, finally the two men inside relinquished their guns and slowly slid from the vehicle.

Cade hurried his pace. "Is anyone in the backseat?"

One of the deputies shook his head, leaned in and popped the trunk.

A few yards away, Cade saw a still body in it, partially covered with a blanket. Sweat broke out on his forehead as he reached the rear of the car.

NINE

Michelle flew out of the car trunk and hugged Cade. "You saved me."

Holding his daughter for the first time with her knowing the truth robbed him of words. He was full of emotions he'd never experienced. His child was safe.

"Let's go. Your mom will be anxious to know you're okay."

Michelle's expression morphed into a scowl. "I don't want to talk with her."

"You might not, but I'm sure she wants to talk to you. You leaving the cabin scared her. Scared Uncle Ben and me too. You could have been killed." He waved his hand toward the pickup. "Time to leave. Your mom has to go to court."

"This trial has taken over our lives. I hate her job." Michelle charged toward the truck.

Cade followed. He didn't want the judge to postpone the trial. It kept Tory in the public eye. Having to go to court every day put Tory in jeopardy until he could solve who was after her and their daughter.

Before getting into the truck, Cade called the land-line at the cabin. No one answered. Was Michelle's kidnapping a diversion so the biker gang could really come after Tory? He paused outside the pickup and punched in Paul's work number.

"No one answered at the cabin. Did you contact Tory or Ben? Are they with you?" he asked immediately when Paul answered. Cade's adrenaline continued to pump through his body, keeping him alert in case there was another kidnapping.

"Yes, to both questions. I was afraid the cabin was compromised so I had Ben drive Tory to the diner. There were enough police swarming the place that I felt she would be safer. Is Michelle safe?"

"Yes. There were three gang members involved. The deputies are bringing them in. I'm heading your way with Michelle. Let Tory know I have—her daughter, and I'll meet her and Uncle Ben at the cabin. We don't have much time to get her to court."

As he drove toward the cabin, Michelle hugged the passenger door as if she was going to jump from the pickup any second. She stared a hole in the dashboard, her arms crisscrossed.

"Why didn't you tell me you were my father last week?" Michelle asked in a whisper as she glanced at him.

Tears glistened in her eyes. The sight of them ripped through him. "I promised your mom I wouldn't."

"Why?"

He wasn't sure how to answer that. There was no answer he could give that wouldn't cause pain. "I didn't want to be the cause of problems between you and your mom."

"Are you sure it isn't between you and me? Why didn't you want to be my father?"

"You had a great dad in Derek." He turned into the drive to the cabin. This trip couldn't be over fast enough.

"Yes, but…" Her gaze fell on Tory standing in the doorway with Uncle Ben in front of her.

Knowing Tory, she'd wanted to go out and meet Michelle. This was his uncle's compromise. "Let's get inside. Now that everyone knows our general location, this isn't a safe haven anymore."

"Then where do we go?"

"I'm not sure yet. First we need to get your mother to the courthouse."

Michelle pushed the door open. "Why not back to my house, especially if Mom's part is basically over today."

"It's never over until the verdict, but the critical part of the trial for her case will be finished." Cade headed toward the cabin.

"We're packed and ready to leave," Uncle Ben said as he backed up to allow them to enter.

Tory took a step toward Michelle.

Michelle moved to Cade's side.

Tory stopped. "We'll have to talk later today, Michelle. What you did was dangerous and foolish."

"What about what you did? Let's get this over with." Michelle snatched up her packed duffel bag and headed outside, forcing them to follow quickly.

Cade walked beside Tory while Uncle Ben hurried to keep up with Michelle.

When their daughter slid into the backseat and his uncle shut the car door, Tory slowed her pace and whispered in a harsh voice, "What did you say to her?"

"Nothing about what happened fifteen years ago. Believe me, she is just as mad at me as you." Except for that one moment when she hugged him at the kidnapper's vehicle. Would that be his last hug from his daughter? "She wanted to know why I didn't want to be her father."

"What did you say?"

"Not much. Not the time or place. All three of us need to sit down and talk about it."

"I never wanted that."

"I know." Cade opened her door, closed it when she was in the front passenger seat, then hurried around the front of the SUV, calling the police chief to let him know his plans for the day. Now the real fun would start.

When he pulled up to the police station, he parked by the back door and peered at Michelle. "You and Uncle Ben are staying here. At the moment this should be one of the safest places in El Rio."

As his uncle skirted the SUV, Michelle glanced from the building to Cade, both eyebrows raised. "You're locking me in a jail?"

"Not in a jail. You two will be in Paul's office. Stay put or a holding cell might be where you'll end up."

Michelle gasped.

"Running off like that nearly got you killed and put all of us in danger. I hope you've learned your lesson about following directions."

As his daughter walked slowly to the rear entrance, Tory said, "I hope that's all it takes for her to do as you say."

The fear in Michelle's face when the car trunk was opened gave him encouragement that it might work. "So do I." He pulled away from the police station. "When will Carlos Dietz arrive at the courthouse?"

Tory checked the clock on the dashboard. "In half

an hour. Paul is coordinating with the US Marshals bringing him."

"Good. You'll be there before he shows up. Today I'm sticking to you like glue."

At noon Tory wrapped up her questions for Carlos on the stand and the judge adjourned for lunch. Next, the defense would have its turn to cross-examine the witness. As she walked to the prosecutor's table, she locked eyes with Cade, sitting in the first row. He hadn't left her side the whole morning. Her gaze dropped to his Texas Ranger's star pinned over his heart on his long-sleeve white shirt.

In the past ten days, she'd come to know a side of him she'd never seen as a teenager. He wore his badge with honor and dignity. His presence in the room commanded attention, and signaled caution to every member of Mederos's gang sitting behind their leader. And respect. Three other gang members were in jail right now because of their kidnapping of Michelle. And she knew without a shadow of doubt they would go to prison for their crimes because Cade was the witness and nothing would stop him from testifying.

As people filed out of the courtroom, Tory stuffed all her papers into her briefcase, then turned to find Cade standing close to her. He'd moved quickly and quietly.

"You did a great job of walking Dietz through his testimony."

"Yeah, but this afternoon will be the toughest part. Mederos's attorney will try to make the man out as an unreliable witness who didn't know what he saw that night his son was gunned down."

"You've done a good job preparing him. Let's go

grab lunch in your office. Rachel should have our food for us by now."

"I'm not sure I can eat anything. I won't rest easy until Carlos is finished testifying."

At the back door to the now empty courtroom, Cade poked his head out of the entrance, looking up and down the corridor. "Clear. Let's use the stairs this time."

Ten minutes later she was inside her office on the first floor, sitting on her leather couch, afraid to relax while she tried to force herself to eat some chicken salad. What little she ate ended up in a tight ball in her stomach.

Her secretary was manning the front office making sure no one disturbed her unless there was an emergency.

"I need to call Michelle before I go back into the courtroom, but I'm not looking forward to it." She took a long sip of her sweetened iced tea.

"If it'll make you feel any better, she's doing fine. Uncle Ben told me she's been sleeping on Paul's couch most of the morning."

"I'm at a loss about what to do with her. In the past, we always had a good relationship. It changed a little when Derek died, but she didn't openly disobey what she was supposed to do."

"I imagine she's scared. The break-in at your house brought your job to your front door. That's hard to ignore."

Yes, she knew that, and when this trial was over, she knew she needed to make a decision. She loved her job, but her daughter was more important.

"Call Uncle Ben. If she's still sleeping, wait. She's got to be exhausted."

"I sure am, and I wasn't sneaking out of the cabin like she was." Tory took another bite of her salad, and managed to chew it although it seemed tasteless. "I might as well call her now."

While she punched in Ben's number, Cade received a call. He stepped outside to answer his phone. When Ben answered, she asked, "Is Michelle awake?"

"No, she paced for the first part of the morning. I think she finally wore herself out."

"Everything okay?"

"A lot is going on here with the three prisoners."

"Are they talking?"

"No, but Paul just came in and told me one of them was involved in your break-in. His fingerprints, previously not in the system, now are, and they matched the ones taken in the bathroom. Paul is in with him. He's new to the gang and might take a deal to flip on Mederos."

"How about the other two? Anything?"

"They asked for their lawyers immediately. Not a word yet."

"Tell Michelle I called to see how she was doing."

"I will. Hang in there."

As Tory put her cell phone down next to her lunch, Cade entered. "That was Paul. He thinks there's a chance one of the kidnappers will talk."

"I heard. Which one?"

"Leon Blackwell. He's only been with the gang for about six months. He was in the passenger seat of the car. He told Paul he had no idea Tomas Jones, the driver, was going to take the girl. When prompted to say more, he clammed up and said he wouldn't talk without a deal and protection."

"Do you think he knows about Carlos making it to testify against Mederos and that he's being given a new life?"

"It's possible. It would be huge if we could weaken the biker gang."

"I hope so. If you hear anything while I'm in court, let me know."

"Paul emphasized that Dietz is alive and well and that he'll be able to start over someplace. A new beginning. That can be tempting for some."

"Paul must have told you about a set of fingerprints that matched ones in my bathroom. Whose prints were they?"

"Leon Blackwell. He'll have a lot to answer for."

"I'd love to put him in prison and throw away the keys. These past couple of weeks have been awful. I've been a DA for years and never had to deal with something like this, but if he can help us bring down Mederos and his gang, then…" Her voice faded into silence. Deals were made all the time in order to convict a criminal like Mederos.

Cade took the seat next to her on the couch. He slid his arm around her shoulders. "If you're not going to eat, then at least try to rest. We have half an hour before we have to be back in court."

She didn't move from his embrace, but even when she closed her eyes and breathed deeply, tension gripped every part of her.

"Relax, Tory. Don't worry about what might happen. Let God take care of it."

Still within his embrace, she lounged back and rested her head on the cushion. Slowly the tightness in her muscles eased. *Lord, that's all I can do right now. Trust You.*

Sleep descended.

Cade tried not to raise his hopes too high, but he'd received a text from Paul Drake that Blackwell wanted to make a deal. He was sending two officers to be in the courtroom. Then they would bring Tory to the police station if he was still interviewing the biker.

When he let Tory know what was happening, she smiled for the first time today. He left when his two replacements appeared and took their positions in the courtroom. Maybe he would have good news by the time she finished. So far Mederos's attorney hadn't been able to sway Dietz to change his testimony nor had the lawyer been able to discredit the grieving father. The man's love for his son came across in each of his replies.

Ten minutes later, Cade entered the back of the police station and immediately headed for Paul's office. He knocked then went into the room. Michelle sat next to Uncle Ben on the couch with a notebook open.

"Homework?" Cade asked as his daughter looked up.

She nodded, then lowered her head as though she were engrossed in the algebra problem.

"Since Tory forgot to bring her math book to the ranch, Paul picked it up when he went by Tory's house to check to make sure the new alarm system was in place," Ben said.

"Does that mean we get to go home today?" Michelle asked while still keeping her head down.

"Yes." Tory could still be in danger, but the star witness had done his damage to Mederos's case already and would be shortly on his way to a new life.

Uncle Ben stood and stretched. "You're early. Are you and Tory finished for the day?"

"She's still at the courthouse. But it should wrap up in the next hour. Two officers are watching her and will bring her to the station."

Michelle looked up. "You left Mom at the courthouse? Why?"

"She's well guarded. Her usefulness to Mederos has been defused today when her star witness testified, but even with that, Tory is being protected." He glanced from Michelle to his uncle. "I'm here to conduct an interview with one of the men in the car this morning."

Michelle stiffened, her pencil falling onto her notebook, then rolling off to land on the couch.

Cade picked up the pencil and sat next to Michelle. "This is a good thing. The more we know the how and why of what went down, the better off we are."

Uncle Ben opened the door. "I'm gonna get some coffee. Be back in a few minutes."

"One of them stunk. I don't think he's taken a bath in weeks. He tossed me into the trunk like I was trash."

Most likely Tomas Jones.

"But the other one smiled at me and told me not to worry right before he closed the trunk. I don't think he liked how the others behaved."

"Did he say or do anything else?"

"No, everything happened so fast. I came around the side of the diner and suddenly was grabbed from behind with a stinky, dirty hand over my mouth, dragged to a car and stuffed into the trunk. I… I…" She swallowed hard.

"Michelle, those men will pay for their crime. They won't be able to hurt you. We caught them in the act."

He didn't know how she would react, but he needed to comfort her. He put his arm around her and held her. "Anytime you want to talk about the abduction, I'll listen, but I hope you'll talk with your mother and maybe a counselor."

She shivered. "All I want to do is forget it."

"I know, but you still need to process it. When I was in the army, I saw a lot and all I wanted to do was forget. The thing is, the memories wouldn't let me go until I dealt with my feelings."

Michelle sighed. "What if you feel overwhelmed?"

"Take it one step at a time. When I tried to force myself, it didn't work. And remember what worked for me, might not for you, but in the end you have to do something." He'd let his experiences in the Middle East override everything else to the point he nearly shut down. It had taken him a long time to admit there was a problem and seek help from the army chaplain.

The door opened and Uncle Ben came into the room with a cup of coffee and a drink for Michelle. "Paul needs you in the interview room."

Cade left the police chief's office with mixed feelings. All he could do was tell his daughter how he handled stress and emotions that twisted him up inside. He didn't have any experience in the dad department, but now that Michelle knew the truth, he wanted to be there for her.

He met Paul in the hallway outside the interview room. "How do you want to do this?"

"He'll get a deal for a new identity in the Witness Protection Program. He'll have to wear an ankle monitor for three years with his movements restricted. But only if the evidence he gives us helps to convict Mederos and the other two involved in the kidnapping. And if he deviates from the agreement, he'll be sent to prison."

At least Blackwell wouldn't get off scot-free. "Okay. Let's get this over with. The more members that go to prison, the harder it will be for the gang to function with their leader gone too."

"I agree and we can put pressure on the ones that are left."

Paul opened the door and went inside first, taking the chair across from the suspect. Cade sat beside Leon, a skinny kid with dark hair and eyes. He grasped his shackled hands together to hide the quivering, but the eighteen-year-old couldn't cover the fear. It poured off him.

"Normally the DA would be in on this plea bargain, but she's in court and the girl you took this morning is her daughter. Ranger Cade Morgan is here instead." Paul stated the terms of the agreement. "Where is your lawyer?"

"I don't got one. That guy that came earlier works for Mederos."

"We can give you a court appointed one." Paul set his elbows on the table and laced his fingers together.

"I waive my rights to a lawyer. I don't wanna stay in El Rio any longer than I hafta."

Paul slid the paper toward Leon, then laid a pen down next to it. "If you need me to read it to you, I can."

Blackwell frowned. "I know how."

"Good. While you're going over the plea bargain, I'll contact the US Marshals. If you provide all the information we need, they will take you somewhere safe tonight. Then you'll only return to El Rio to testify when the time comes." Paul rose and left Cade with the prisoner.

After he read the document, Cade gave him another. "If you're giving up your rights to talk to a lawyer before taking the plea bargain, I need you to sign this paper stating that first."

When the paperwork was taken care of, Cade set the signed sheets to the side. "This interview is being recorded."

"Fine. Let's get this over with. Mederos has men everywhere."

"At the police station?"

Blackwell shrugged. "Maybe but I don't know nothing for sure. If I was him, I'd have a cop or two on the payroll."

"I don't want any speculation. I want the truth. Things you know for sure."

"Sure. Just saying the guy is smart and mean as a rattlesnake."

Cade withdrew a piece of paper from the folder Paul left on the table. "Can you explain how your fingerprints were found inside District Attorney Carson's house in her daughter's bathroom?" He passed the young man the sheet with his prints on it.

Blackwell shrugged. "We dinna have a lot of time. I got sloppy."

"Who sent you to that place?"

"I don't know. Pedro asked me to go with him."

"So Mederos's brother was at the house too?"

Blackwell nodded. "I don't have a beef with the lady."

"But someone does? Who? Pedro?"

"I guess so. He dinna like his bro in jail."

Cade flipped through the folder and produced the photo left on Tory's pillow. "Where did you get this?"

"Pedro had it when we left the courtroom at noon. We were gonna trash the whole place, but the lady came home. We had to hightail it out of there."

"So you didn't plan to confront her and her daughter?" Cade squeezed his hand into a fist.

"No. Just scare her."

"How did you know she wouldn't be home right after the trial?"

"Pedro heard her talking earlier about going to her daughter's high school basketball game. She was supposed to be there."

"You came in and out of the bedroom window?"

"Yep."

"So far you haven't told us anything we don't already know. One of your fingerprints was in the pig's blood in the bathroom. If you don't give us something of value, then there's no deal."

"I said I'd talk about what I know."

"So were you part of Judge Parks's kidnapping and death?"

Blackwell's eyes grew round. "No way. None of us were."

"How about Pedro? His fingerprints were on the tailgate's handle."

"Pedro and me were gettin' stinkin' drunk at the garage. A few others were there with their gals."

"If you think they'll be an alibi for you and Pedro, think again," Cade said.

"They dinna leave until Buck showed up the next morning."

"Joe Buckner, Mederos's right-hand guy?"

"Yep. Wasn't too happy with us."

"Why?"

"'Cuz Mederos was mad at us for tearin' apart the lady's place."

"So he didn't tell his brother to trash the house?"

"Nope. We messed up his plans."

"What plans?" Frustration knotted Cade's gut. This wasn't going to help him get to the bottom of what was going on.

Blackwell lifted his shoulders in a shrug. "Pedro dinna know either."

"Where's Pedro then?"

"Dunno. He went with Buck, and I never saw him again."

Cade's patience shredded at Blackwell's nonchalant attitude. Obviously he didn't understand what making a deal meant. Cade brought his fist down on the table between them. The teenager jerked back. "You lying—"

He shook his head, his long hair flying all over the place. "I ain't. I dunno. Just ask Pedro when ya find him."

"*If* I find him. Do you have any idea where he would go? It sounds like you two were friends." He wasn't going to leave this room until he got something useful out of Blackwell.

"He has a girlfriend. Kara Myers. I don't know if he's there, but they were tight. She lives on a ranch between here and San Antonio with her grandparents."

"Who else knows about her and Pedro?"

"No one. She's different from women who hang around usually. Pedro was thinkin' of leavin' the gang. He was tryin' to get his nerve to say somethin' to his bro."

He decided to move on to the kidnapping. "I'll check it out. Tell me how you and Jones ended up at the diner. It wasn't by coincidence."

"Buck got a call, then sent us there to take the girl."

My daughter! Cade's anger overwhelmed him again. He could be tough with a suspect, but throughout his career he'd learned kindness and calmness worked better. He shoved down the rising fury. "Who called?"

"I—I—dunno." Blackwell looked toward the camera mounted on the wall, then leaned toward Cade and whispered in such a low voice Cade barely heard the teenager. "Turn off the recording."

He assessed Blackwell. His gaze flitted from one place to another. His breathing was shallow, and his hands twisted together over and over. Fear took hold of the teen.

Cade rose and went to the camera and flipped it off. "This takes care of the video and audio feed." When he retook his chair, fear still held Blackwell as though a vise had clamped around him. "What are you afraid of?"

"The US Marshals will pick me up right away? I won't have to stay in this jail tonight?"

"Yes. They're on their way from San Antonio."

"The caller was Mederos's informant inside the police department." Blackwell kept his voice low. "He's the only one who knows his identity, but Buck has dealt with the person over the phone since Mederos went to jail."

TEN

"Is the informant a police officer?" Cade bent closer, realizing the danger Blackwell was in.

"Not sure. I think so. It's a man 'cuz Buck said *he* when referring to the informant. That's why I wanna talk to only you. I can't stay here." Sweat rolled down the teen's face.

"We'll need you to testify to what you know. Any details you can think of about the informant, let me know. When he called. Something you've overheard Mederos or Buck say in reference to him."

"I'm not in the inner circle. I've only picked up bits and pieces since I joined the gang six months ago. I think Pedro knows who the mole is, but he never said who."

The police would need evidence to back up what the teenager was telling Cade. He would have to trust Paul with what was going on. He needed someone in the police department to help him check the employees at the station. He didn't think his friend was the informant, but he couldn't rule out anyone 100 percent. "Why did you and Jones take the girl?"

"To stall the witness's testimony. The informant was

trying to find out where Dietz was being kept and had narrowed down the area. That's what Jones told me. Buck received the call this morning at seven on his cell. Buck went into the other room at the garage then came out and told us what to do."

"Do you know anything else about the informant?"

"I once heard Mederos tell Buck the informant was the reason he came to El Rio. He owed Mederos 'cuz of somethin' when they were teenagers."

"What?"

"He never said."

Cade would go to Judge Duggin and get a warrant for Buck's cell phone records. Maybe something would pan out. He could also look into anyone working for the police who might have a connection to Mederos when they grew up, someone who wasn't originally from here. At least he could rule out Paul who'd lived in El Rio his whole life. "Where were you taking your hostage?"

"To an abandoned house in San Antonio."

"Why that far?"

"You'll have to ask Buck that. I don't think Jones knew. He told me he was following orders."

"Did you burn my barn down and start a grass fire?"

Blackwell shook his head. "But Tomas and Buck left the garage that night. I saw them put some gallon cans in the back of a car. I don't know though for sure they set your barn on fire."

Cade shoved to his feet. That would be a question to ask Tomas. "I'll be back in a minute. I want to make sure everything is set for your—"

"No, you can't leave me alone here! I've helped you. You gotta help me."

"I'm just going to the main room to check on something." Besides seeing when the US Marshals would arrive, he wanted to make sure Tory was back from the courtroom and was okay.

Blackwell jumped to his feet and jerked on the chains anchoring him to the table. Terror ravished the teen's face. "Take me with you!"

Cade moved back to the table and placed his hand on the teen's shoulder. "Sit. I'll stay."

Tory strolled into the police station, flanked by two officers. Tired but elated that the defense had finished questioning Carlos today, and her witness was being transported back to his safe house, soon to leave for a new life. Now all she wanted to do was hug Michelle and never let her go.

Paul led her to his office past one gang member— Tomas Jones—and opened the door for her. When she stepped inside, Michelle leaped from the couch and threw her arms around Tory.

"I'm sorry, Mom. I wasn't thinking this morning."

"I know, baby." The feel of Michelle clasped against her soothed her anxiety. All the way through the trial today, she had to force herself to focus on what was going on in the courtroom. But for the time being she needed to forget her job and center on her daughter. They had to talk about what Michelle had discovered. "Are you ready to go home?"

Her daughter nodded and started gathering her bag.

Tory glanced at Ben. "Where's Cade? I thought he would be in here with you all."

"For the past two hours, he's been in the interview room with a suspect. He shouldn't be too much longer."

Which kidnapper was he interviewing? The guy who

wanted the deal or one of the other two? As much as she wanted to know, she would spend time with Michelle and wait on Cade. Her job was to prosecute—Cade's was to apprehend. She needed to respect those boundaries and mend her family.

Tory sat on the couch and patted the cushion next to her. "Tell me what you've been working on today."

Beside her, Michelle showed her the schoolwork she'd done. "It's not much. I slept half the day."

"Did you get any rest last night?"

Michelle shook her head. "I was too mad."

"I'm sorry, honey. I was only six years older than you when I made that decision. It seemed like the right one at the time." Tory looked at Ben. "Now I don't know that it was."

"But remember that time I asked you if I was adopted because a friend was and you told me no."

"Which is true. You weren't adopted." All Tory wanted to do was keep Michelle close to her.

"But Dad wasn't my father."

"In his heart he was. He raised you, loved you and cared for you as if you were. He wanted to be a father so badly and you were his one chance at being a dad."

"He couldn't have children?"

"No, but when he found that out, he only told me. Grandpa and Grandma Carson don't know that he couldn't."

Ben cleared his throat. "I'll go try and rush my nephew along."

When the door closed behind Ben, Michelle rubbed her hands together, something she did when she was nervous. "I don't know if I can think of anyone else as my dad."

"I'm not asking you to, and I don't think Cade is either."

"He saved me today." Michelle shuddered and crossed her arms as though the temperature had suddenly plunged. "I was so scared in the trunk. I saw Cade come into the diner and knew he was there for me. I hurried to the bathroom and crawled out the window. Then everything happened so fast. I tried to fight. But I couldn't."

Tory remembered seeing Tomas Jones being guarded by Officer McKay. Tomas was big, muscular and frightening with a lot of his body covered in tattoos—one being a skull and crossbones prominently showcased on his arm as all members of the biker gang had. "Honey, you have to decide what you're comfortable with."

"If I hadn't overheard y'all talking, would you have ever told me who Cade was?"

"Honestly, I don't know. Cade and I haven't really talked about the future much."

"Do you love him?"

"I can't answer that."

"Why not?"

"Because all I've been doing is living one day at a time ever since our house was broken into. My feelings are all jumbled up."

Michelle stood and stared at her. "Did you love him once?"

"Very much."

"Dad?"

"I loved him too."

"How can you love two men at the same time?"

Tory felt as though she were in the witness box being drilled by a prosecutor. "My love for Derek was different than what I felt for Cade. I'm not going to kid you. When I married Derek, we were great friends. He will always have a special place in my heart. We—I grew to love him."

Michelle's eyes clouded. "He didn't love you?"

"No, he did. I think that's why he wanted to marry me. He told me after a few years he never regretted marrying me."

Michelle massaged her fingertips into her temples. "This is so much to take in."

"Baby, I want you to take your time. I don't want you to feel pressured into feeling something you don't." Right after her wedding to Derek, she'd felt guilty that she couldn't forget Cade. Finally after several years, thoughts of Cade had faded—only to return when he came back.

Does that mean I still love him?

A light rap on the door sounded followed by it being opened. Cade gave them a tired smile. "Are y'all ready to go to your home? Uncle Ben is already planning what he's fixing for dinner."

"What?" Michelle asked, almost shyly with her gaze lowering.

"My kind of food. Steak, baked potato and a salad. Easy and delicious."

Tory slung her arm over Michelle's shoulders. "I'm starving. We'll have to stop at the grocery store to get a few supplies."

"Uncle Ben already suggested that. We'll wait outside. He told me he could fly through the place and get what he wants in ten minutes."

Tory released a long breath. "Not having to cook this past ten days has been a treat for me."

As Tory emerged from the police chief's office, she caught a glimpse of Leon Blackwell being escorted out the rear of the building with two men. Her gaze rested on Cade. "US Marshals?"

He nodded. "We're in a good place."

Tory wanted to believe that and relax, but she couldn't let go of the tension she'd endured the past couple of weeks. It still dug deep into her.

When the bell rang, Cade started for the front door, but Tory beat him to it.

"Come in, Paul. I was hoping you would stop by and let me know what's happening since Leon Blackwell talked." Tory moved to allow the police chief into her house that evening.

"Buck has been arrested and Tomas Jones has expressed interest in a deal too. Several of the gang members have disappeared. We think they've fled before they were arrested. With the help of Blackwell and Jones we'll be able to take down a lot of gang members." He walked into the living room. "I could have called you with that info, but I haven't felt this optimistic in years. I wanted to share it in person."

"So do you think I'm safe now?" Tory took a chair across from Paul in her living room.

Cade came up beside her. "I'll answer that. As soon as we can account for who murdered Judge Parks and why, as well as who was the sniper on the building behind the courthouse and the incidents at my ranch, then you can breathe easier. Until then I suggest caution." Earlier when Tory and Michelle returned to their home, they both had hung out in the living room or kitchen. Cade was glad his daughter and Uncle Ben were in the utility room helping Bella finally give birth. After dinner that had kept Michelle's mind off what had been done over a week ago to her bedroom and the bathroom.

"Tomas finally admitted to setting your barn on fire and hanging an inflatable doll from the rafters as part of his plea bargaining. But I still agree with Cade about using caution. So far we know Mederos or his gang has been behind the trashing of your house and the attempted kidnapping of Michelle. We're still unclear about the judge and the other shooting at the courthouse. After everything settled down, I had a chat with Mederos again about Judge Parks. As expected, he still denies his gang's, especially his little brother's, involvement."

Tory sat forward. "And the courthouse shooting?"

Paul nodded. "I have Detective Alexander and Officer McKay heading to speak with Kara Myers about Pedro. Sheriff deputies are backing them up in case Pedro is there and tries to flee. When arresting Buck, we had a warrant to search the garage where the gang hangs out. We found some guns, but none that fit what was used by the sniper or Judge Parks's murder."

"Were all the weapons legal?" Cade asked and sat in the chair next to Tory. After all the highs and lows of the day, exhaustion set in.

"No and that meant we could take a couple more gang members to jail. We didn't get all." Paul grinned. "It's quite crowded with Mederos and his followers. And I ain't complaining."

Tory finally relaxed against the back chair cushion. "It sounds like we owe Leon for starting the landslide of good news."

"This is when I love my job. I think Mederos in jail awaiting trial has caused some doubts and unrest with the gang. He ruled with an iron fist." Paul rose and started toward the entry hall. "Oh, just as a precaution, I'm keeping an officer outside your house until at least the Mederos trial is over."

"You don't have to. Uncle Ben and I are staying until all the loose ends are tied up." Cade couldn't explain why he felt there was more going on than what had been revealed. He hoped that Detective Alexander brought in Pedro and that he would confess to the murder.

Paul paused at the front door. "Are y'all going to stay in town here or go back to the ranch?"

Cade stepped closer. "I don't know. The only part of my house damaged was the garage, which I have people coming to fix. Michelle still hasn't gone down the hall to the bedrooms and bathroom. This might not be a good place for her right now."

"I can't blame the girl for feeling like that. Let me know if you move."

"Will do." Cade shook Paul's hand. "Thanks for offering an officer outside the house, but I know how stretched you are right now, especially with the extra prisoners at the jail. Right now she's excited about Bella having her puppies. Maybe that'll take her mind off things."

After the police chief left, Cade returned to the living room, stopping a moment in the entrance. Tory laid her head against the side of the wingback, her eyes closed. She looked so tired and vulnerable. The urge to kiss her swamped him. Through the years, he'd dedicated his life to his job, protecting his heart against falling in love a second time. He never wanted to go through that pain again.

He crossed the room and headed for the kitchen.

As he entered, Uncle Ben exclaimed, "That's the last puppy."

"Three pups. I've never seen a live birth before."

The excitement in Michelle's voice drew Cade to the utility room. His uncle and daughter knelt on the floor next to the large cardboard box they had made up for Bella.

Cade approached and looked at the newborn puppies. Bella was licking the last one born.

Michelle looked up at him and beamed. "They're so cute."

"Yep." Seeing the new pups reminded him that life went on in spite of bad things happening all around them.

"I want to sleep in here in case Bella needs me." Her grin grew. "Please."

His heart melted. Emotions he'd tried to deny himself all these years swelled into his throat. He swallowed hard and said, "You need to ask your mother." He was her father, but he still didn't feel he had a right to make decisions concerning Michelle other than safety ones right now. Maybe in the future that would change. The hope that her smile had given him expanded.

Michelle stood. "Where's Mom?"

"In the living room—" his daughter passed him and was across the kitchen before he finished saying "—taking a cat nap."

Uncle Ben chuckled. "A gal on a mission. I think Bella picked the perfect time to have her pups. The past few hours have taken Michelle's mind off what's happening."

"I agree."

"She's talking about having her own puppy. You might say something to Tory."

"Yeah. We still haven't really talked about what everyone avoided mentioning at dinner."

"Give Michelle time to process it all. She hasn't had much time with everything that's going on."

"I don't even know what Tory really thinks. We haven't talked much about the situation now that Michelle knows. We've been dealing with one crisis after another."

"And that doesn't allow either one of you enough time to handle all the feelings I'm sure you're both experiencing. I know how much you loved Tory when you left for your assignment overseas. Those feelings didn't go away overnight. Nor what you felt when you learned of her marriage. Maybe this is your second chance."

At what? Being a father? A husband? To have a deeper relationship than casual? "I'd better go see what Tory has decided about where Michelle will sleep."

"You know it's an avoidance tactic on Michelle's part. She doesn't want to sleep in her bedroom alone."

"Yes."

Cade made his way to the living room. The sound of Tory's and his daughter's voices drifted to him. At least there wasn't any shouting. That was a good sign.

"I don't know, Michelle. You'll be sleeping on the hard floor." Tory glanced at him.

"How about that blow-up mattress we have? I really want to do it. What if something happened to Bella or one of the puppies?"

Tory's forehead scrunched. "I'm not sure where I put it."

"It's in the garage with the camping equipment we

used when Grandpa and Grandma took us to Big Bend National Park."

"If you want, I'll go with her and bring it inside the house." Cade leaned against the entrance into the living room, suddenly wanting to avoid what needed to be discussed. He wasn't an indecisive person, and it was strange to find himself doing a task rather than sitting down and getting the inevitable over with.

Tory leaned forward. "If you're sure, Michelle, it's fine with me, but you'll have to go to your bedroom soon. Paul and my secretary made sure everything was put back in place. We have a state-of-the-art alarm system with sensors on each window, and Cade and Ben will be here for a few days. We're safe."

Did she feel that way? A forcefulness to her words made Cade question that last sentence, but maybe Michelle didn't hear it. Tory certainly was trying to put up a brave front, but there were still a lot of unanswered questions in this case.

Michelle blew out a huff of air. "I'll never go back into that room. I'll sleep in the living room, kitchen, anywhere but in there. I'd never get any rest otherwise."

"Okay, the utility room it is for tonight." Tory's troubled gaze met his.

"We'll be back in a minute." Cade let Michelle go first, throwing a glance over his shoulder at Tory as he left.

Tory collapsed back in the chair, her head down, her shoulders hunched.

"Michelle, have Uncle Ben go with you," Cade said and moved back into the living room. He cut the distance to Tory and knelt by her chair. "You aren't alone anymore, Tory. Michelle doesn't have to think of me as her father, but I hope she'll allow me to be in her life as a friend."

Peering at him, Tory sighed. "Michelle often doesn't know what she wants. I can't blame her about not going into her bedroom. If that had happened in mine, I wouldn't either."

"You have a spare one. Let her use it."

"I'm not even sure she'll want to do that. I've been in this house for fifteen years. It has been my home for a long time, but maybe I'll need to consider moving."

"It's nothing you have to decide right now. Time has a way of changing our perspective."

She gave him a half smile. "Yes, I'm beginning to see that. For so long I was mad at you for what happened between us, but now I see that circumstances, some beyond our control, got in the way. We weren't meant to be together back then."

"I'm beginning to think we've been given a second chance." He finally said what he'd been thinking for the past twenty-four hours.

"Possibly. But we shouldn't rush into anything. Thankfully what's going on right now isn't our usual life. I feel overwhelmed in every area of my life. I can't make a good decision feeling that way."

"Neither can I." He clasped her hand, relishing the link with her. "We should postpone the discussion of what's next with our daughter until everything is back to normal."

She chuckled. "I'm not sure if we're both being chicken or brilliant in that conclusion."

"I want to believe brilliant."

Sounds of Michelle coming into the living room

prompted Cade to release Tory's hand and stand. "What's brilliant?"

"Your idea about the blow-up mattress. Did you see the other one in the garage?" Tory rose and started for the hallway.

"Yes. Do you want Uncle Ben and me to get that one too?"

At the living room entrance, Tory paused. "Yes. We all might as well camp out in the living room. That'll leave the couch free for whoever isn't on guard duty. That person can check on Bella and her puppies. I'm going to get the bedding we'll need."

As Tory disappeared down the hallway, Michelle murmured, "How can she go back there alone?"

"She won't be." Although Tory probably didn't need any help, Cade strode after her.

Tory had already set some sheets and blankets on the floor in front of the linen closet. "I can get this."

"I know. Michelle was concerned that you were alone back here."

"I've decided that when this trial is over, I'm going to look for another place to live. Michelle has enough to deal with. The house doesn't need to be an issue."

"I'll help you anyway I can." Maybe both Tory and Michelle starting over in a new home would make it easier to be part of Michelle's life.

"Since you're here—" Tory handed him all the blankets "—you can help me with these. I'll get some pillows."

A half an hour later, two mattresses and the couch were made up as beds. Michelle went to see Bella before going to sleep.

Cade looked at Uncle Ben. He was feeling his age,

his movements slower. "I'm taking the first watch." Cade intended to let his uncle get some extra rest, but he wouldn't tell him that. Uncle Ben refused to think of himself as getting older. Age was all in a person's mind. But after watching him, Cade knew it was also in the body.

As his uncle, Tory and Michelle settled down to sleep, Cade inspected all the windows and doors, then walked into the kitchen to make a pot of coffee. Earlier he'd brought in the files to see if anything jumped out at him, but he wasn't sure how much he'd get done. His body, but worse his mind, was tired.

After staring at the same sheet of paper for five minutes, he got up and went into the utility room. He needed a distraction, and Bella and her puppies fit the bill. He sat on the floor by the cardboard box. His dog lifted her head and rested it on the top edge.

"I've got a feeling we're both worn out." Cade rubbed Bella behind the ears. "You did good, girl. Now if only I can tie up all the loose ends. I certainly can't take Mederos's word he didn't have the judge killed or Officer Sims shot."

Cade lounged against the washing machine, stroking Bella. The action, along with observing the three puppies rooting around, relaxed him.

Until a shout slashed the silence. *Get away!*

ELEVEN

The overhead light flooded the living room with brightness. Tory's eyes blinked open as she fought—the sheets that encased her.

Suddenly Cade stood over her. "Are you okay?"

Tory looked to the right and saw Michelle's wide gaze on her. When she glanced at Ben on the couch, a confused expression carved deep lines into his face.

Cade knelt next to her mattress. "Tory, you screamed."

She struggled beneath the twisted sheet and finally managed to sit up. "Sorry. Bad dream. I was fighting a dark shadow."

"Mom, aren't we safe here?"

She wanted to say no, but they were as safe as they could be in El Rio. She didn't want Michelle to live in fear, and yet she wanted her thinking before reacting like earlier today. "Yes, we're safe. I'm just overtired, honey." She waved her hand toward Cade, inches from her. "See. Cade was in here right away. He's good at his job."

"Yeah, I'm here because he does a good job."

Tory had never seen Cade blush, but he did when

Michelle smiled at him. It looked like she wasn't mad at him any longer, but Tory wasn't so sure her daughter wasn't angry at her. And Tory understood why. Fear made her doubt Cade all those years ago, and she took the easy way out.

"Okay, y'all. I'm gonna stand guard in a while and I need my beauty sleep." Ben punched his pillow and settled back on the couch.

"So do I. I have court tomorrow." Tory leaned over and hugged Michelle. "Sorry to scare you, honey."

As Michelle pulled her covers up over her shoulder, Tory looked at Cade—so close she could bend toward him and kiss him. She wanted to. In his eyes he wanted her to, but she didn't. She wouldn't get any sleep if she did. "Good night, Cade."

Cade closed the door to Paul's office and sat in the chair in front of the police chief's desk. "Detective Alexander told me they came up empty. Pedro wasn't there. Even Kara was gone to a friend's. Mr. Myers didn't know who Kara was with so he was probably covering for her. The old man did let them search the ranch. Nothing. No indication Pedro was ever there."

"Yup. That about sums it up. And even better, Tomas Jones confirmed that he had to rally Pedro and Leon after a night of drinking at the garage. He left them there the night before about twelve and came back early in the morning to find them passed out on the couch. The time of death for Judge Parks was between five and seven p.m. He was killed not long after he left the courthouse."

"Yeah, the evidence at his house fits with that. He came home from work but hadn't changed yet to go camping. His gear was packed and by the door in the kitchen. I'm not even sure he was in the house long before he was attacked. So if Pedro didn't kill the judge, then why were his fingerprints on the tailgate of the stolen truck where the judge was killed?"

"Good question. We have to find him." Paul sat forward in his desk chair. "Any suggestions who the mole is at the station?"

"No, but with Jones's and Blackwell's testimony, Buck will stand trial for kidnapping and arson. He's the one that sent the three to take Michelle. Maybe he'll see the wisdom in giving up the guy for a shorter sentence. A crooked cop feeding info to a gang leader like Mederos needs to go away for a long time. No telling what he has been responsible for."

"Do you think it's the same guy? What if the cop killed the judge for Mederos?"

"Anything is possible, but I don't think Judge Parks's death would have made a difference in how the trial has proceeded. Something else is going on." If only Cade could figure out what it was because Tory and Michelle were still in danger. What sleep he had gotten last night was riddled with nagging doubts, but nothing he could pinpoint.

Paul stood. "Maybe we can find Pedro. If Blackwell is right and Mederos's little brother knows who the mole is, we might find out that way. But right now, I'm going to have another crack at Buck about the police mole."

"Do you want me to come?"

"No, I need Pedro brought in. Find Kara Myers. Talk with Detective Alexander about her whereabouts. He was tracking down her friends."

Cade nodded and left Paul's office right behind him.

When he scanned the station, he didn't see the detective, but Lieutenant Sanders was at his desk. He headed for the man who had originally arrested Mederos.

"Do you know where Detective Alexander went?"

"He went to talk to one of Kara Myers's friends. He said something about going to where she worked at Taylor's Feed Store."

"Thanks. Has he discovered any info about Pedro's whereabouts?"

"No, but not from lack of trying. If anyone can, he will. He's like a pit bull when he gets on a case."

"I'll see if I can track him down." Cade made his way to his SUV in the back parking lot. As he slid behind the steering wheel, he glanced at the time. He needed to be in the courtroom for Tory by lunchtime. Although there were two guards for her, he didn't totally trust anyone but himself to protect her.

His cell phone rang. When he looked at the number, he didn't recognize it. "Morgan here."

Silence greeted him.

"Who's there?" he asked.

He almost disconnected the call when a quavering voice said, "This is Kara Myers. Pedro told me to call you if I needed help."

"Where are you?"

"Safe for now. I know where Pedro was hiding out. He hasn't contacted me in days. I think he's in trouble."

"Why do you say that?"

"Because he didn't meet me last night like he was supposed to. Gramps told me to stay away. He thinks something is wrong. I don't know what to do."

Cade felt the same way. Something was wrong. "Have you gone to Pedro's hideout?"

"Yes, once. I'm scared." Kara's voice quavered. "Pedro said if anything happened to him, I should call you. You weren't the mole in the police department."

"Where is the hideout?"

"I can show you if you'll pick me up. I don't know where to hide. I need your help."

"I'll protect you. Where are you?"

After she told him, he put the car into Drive. "I'm coming."

As he headed for the vacant house, his phone rang again. This time it was Tory. He asked her, "Are you breaking early for lunch?"

"Things moved faster this morning than I thought. Sam White and I gave our closing statements a while ago. Now the jury is deliberating the verdict. I don't know how long this will be. I can have the guards escort me to my office if you want. I should be safe there."

"No, I'll pick you up. I've got a break concerning Pedro. Kara Myers knows where he is."

"I'm going with you. No way am I sitting this out," Tory said as Cade climbed behind the wheel and started the SUV.

"I don't want you involved."

"Involved? I'd say I'm smack dab in the middle of all of this. I want to know who the mole is. There have been several gang members' cases falling apart unexpectedly. Probably because of the mole."

"You need to do exactly what I say. Agree?"

"Yes. Believe me I don't want to be in danger, but I need answers."

Cade didn't reply to her remark but instead kept his focus on the road before him. His hands were gripping the steering wheel so tightly his knuckles were white. He didn't understand. She'd rather be with him than at home wondering what was happening. Too many deaths. Too many unexpected outcomes.

On the outskirts of El Rio, he drove down a street with houses that had weathered hard times. "What if the verdict comes back soon?"

"Then either I'll have to be dropped off at the courthouse or my assistant DA will have to stand in for me. The verdict will be what it is. My presence won't change it. We need to finish this."

"We? I wouldn't be bringing you if I thought you would sit by quietly and let me meet Kara alone. I wouldn't put it past you to follow me in your car."

She smiled. The thought had crossed her mind. Her Chevy was sitting in her garage where it had been delivered after the mechanic fixed the cut brake line. "Maybe. I like to keep you on your toes."

He chuckled. "If I didn't think you were safe sitting in this armored SUV, I would drag you to the police station and have Paul guard you."

Cade drove into the driveway of a small white clapboard house and pulled around back where he parked. "Stay put. I should only be a minute. Kara is coming with us after I check for weapons. She's going to take us to Pedro's hideout."

"Always the suspicious cop."

"Yes. Part of my job."

While he was gone, Tory phoned her secretary to have her call Tory's cell number if a verdict was reached before she returned to the courthouse. By the time she finished her brief exchange with Rachel, Cade hurried out of the house with a petite young redhead. She appeared as if she were no more than eighteen or nineteen. As she neared, Tory glimpsed the fear in her expression, her gaze darting all around. When she slipped into the backseat, she lowered her head and her long hair fell forward, blocking part of her face.

"I'm Tory Carson. I'm glad you're going to help us."

"He told me you were the DA." Kara's eyes remained down.

"Yes. We're working on this case together." While Cade settled behind the steering wheel, Tory asked, "Where's Pedro?"

"In an abandoned warehouse this side of San Antonio," Cade answered for Kara. "We should be there in half an hour. She won't tell me more until we are out of El Rio and we aren't being followed."

"I like your caution." When Kara met her gaze, Tory smiled at her.

"I'm afraid Pedro is dead." The young woman's hands trembled. She clasped them together.

Tory tried to get Kara to talk and relax, but as Tory talked the scarier Pedro's girlfriend became. Finally Tory stopped, but kept her body turned so she could observe Kara. After all, she was dating a member of a biker gang. What if this was a setup?

Cade circled the small warehouse and found a door unlocked. As he entered the dimly lit premise, he pulled his gun from his holster. The farther he moved away from the entrance a rotten scent assaulted his senses. Something died in here. He hoped it was a rodent, but as the smell grew more nauseating, it didn't bode well for Pedro or someone else.

A door ajar at the back of the warehouse drew him.

He checked every nook and crevice as he crept closer. The repugnant odor seeping into every orifice roiled his gut. When he stepped into the room, his gaze zeroed in on the male hanging by his arms from the rafter, tortured and almost unrecognizable. The black blood-matted hair fit Pedro's color and the build was the same, but otherwise he couldn't tell if it was him.

He approached the dead body and circled it. Its wallet stuck out of its back jean pocket. After easing it out, he flipped it open and found Pedro Mederos's driver's license, along with hundreds of dollars. It wasn't robbery, but then the state he was left indicated his assailant wanted something else from him. What? Blackwell thought that Pedro knew who the police mole was. Did someone else want that name too? Or was this the work of the traitor?

Cade took out his cell phone and snapped pictures of Pedro and the surrounding room. Anything odd he took a photograph, from a toothpick on the floor not far from the body to an old, bloody rag at the door. Then he placed a call to the San Antonio Police Department and the Texas Rangers headquarters in town.

He left the warehouse, dreading the next thing he needed to do. Tell Kara Pedro was dead. Instead of sliding behind the steering wheel, Cade sat in the backseat and twisted to face Kara.

Before he could say anything, the redhead said, "Pedro's dead."

"Yes, I've notified the police. We need to stay until they arrive. I have another Texas Ranger coming out to work the case with the SAPD. He'll keep me informed of the case."

"How—how…" Kara's voice choked. Tears flooded her eyes, and she looked down.

"He was shot." But he wouldn't tell her multiple times. She didn't need that to deal with on top of losing her boyfriend.

Kara buried her face in her hands and cried. Cade wasn't sure what to do. He glanced at Tory.

"Let me sit back there."

Her offer sent relief through him. He always felt awkward comforting a victim's loved one he didn't know. He mouthed the words, "Thank you."

By the time Tory had slipped into the backseat and embraced Kara, two squad cars drove into the parking lot and stopped next to the SUV.

"I shouldn't be long, then we'll return to El Rio." As he climbed from his car, Cade wondered if Kara needed to be protected. Did the killer get the information he wanted? Or would he come after Kara because he thought Pedro had told her something that could get her killed?

While Cade walked the SAPD through the crime scene, one of their police officers stood by his SUV. He showed the detective what he'd found at the pallet in the corner to the rag and the toothpick. "Any DNA found on it, I'd like to know right away as well as the autopsy, especially time of death. I don't think he was here long. There was a fast food bag wadded up on his bedding. No other sign of food."

"How long has he been missing?"

"I've been looking for him ten days. His girlfriend heard from him a week ago. Nothing since then. We have several people still in danger. If you could put a rush on it, I'd appreciate it. In fact, another Texas

Ranger should be here soon. He could use our lab to get a fast turnaround."

"I already heard from Steven Calhoun. He was delayed but will be here shortly. We've worked together before."

Cade wished he could work Pedro's murder, but Steven was a top-notch Texas Ranger investigator. This part of the case was in good hands. "My phone number is on this." Cade gave the detective his business card. "Call whenever you have any information."

He left and strode to the SUV. After thanking the police officer, Cade slid into the driver's seat and glanced at Tory and Kara who was calm now. "Kara, I'd like you to stay with us tonight while I assess if you're in any danger. I believe once the news that Pedro has been found gets out, no one will bother you."

"My daughter will be thrilled to talk to someone nearer her age, so I hope you'll stay at my house. And the best part is Bella delivered three puppies who are adorable."

"I love dogs. If you're sure."

Tory's gaze linked with Cade's. "I am."

Cade drove from the parking lot, and as before when he came to the warehouse, he kept an eye on the vehicles about him. If the mole was an El Rio police officer, he might be monitoring the police channel. He almost welcomed being followed. Then he could end this once and for all.

Finally quiet reigned in Tory's house when Michelle and Kara went to sleep in Tory's bedroom. At first she'd been surprised her daughter would even walk down the hallway, but Ben declared he was going to rest in a real bed and was going to use Michelle's. Michelle and Kara moved Bella and the puppies back to Tory's bedroom so they could watch over them. Tory had agreed but made them promise not to bring the dogs into her bed.

Tory came into the kitchen. Cade's attention glued to the laptop screen, he held up his mug. She detoured, took it and refilled it with freshly brewed coffee. With her own cup full, she sat beside him at the table. "Any progress?"

"I or Uncle Ben have ruled over half the people at the police station out so far. It can be tedious running background checks on so many people, especially when you hear in your mind a clock ticking down."

"Why do you say that?"

"Someone beside us is hunting the mole. I want to get to him before whoever interrogated Pedro does."

"Could the informant have killed Pedro?"

"I don't think so." Cade's gut knotted. "Something else is going on. I'm glad Buck and Mederos are in jail. Paul is keeping an eye on them. From what Blackwell and Jones confirmed, they're the only ones who know who the person is besides Pedro possibly. We still don't know that for sure."

"So why is someone else after the police mole?"

"If I could answer that I think I would know who killed Judge Parks. I've been bothered by his murder from the beginning. It hasn't fit with what else has been happening. Both Jones and Blackwell deny the gang had anything to do with it, yet gave us information on other serious crimes."

"How about Officer Sims's shooting? Your two informants haven't acknowledged anyone from the gang shot at him and me."

Cade cocked his head to the side. "No, which makes me think it wasn't a gang member."

"The same person did both of them?"

"Probably. Possibly in all the incidents happening one on top of another someone wanted to hide his agenda in the middle of the ongoing case. Mederos and his gang are good scapegoats if you want to get away with murder."

"Then we need to refocus on all the cases that had Judge Parks and Officer Sims on them. I can do that while you look for the mole. The list we started may be different if you take me out of the equation. I can access my records from home. I'll go get my briefcase with my work computer in it."

Tory walked toward her bedroom. As she passed the bathroom, she shivered. As soon as life returned to normal, she was going to put the house on the market. Too many memories. She wanted a fresh start for her and Michelle. Maybe even a new job—one not so dangerous. As she passed her photo wall in the hallway, she glimpsed Belinda and her sitting at an outdoor café. But then her best friend had a safe job as a secretary, and she was murdered in a bank robbery. Cade would say she shouldn't worry about what could happen. Instead, savor the moment.

Tory quietly inched the door open and entered her bedroom. Bella looked up at her as she crossed to her closet while Michelle and Kara slept on the king-size bed. She hoped when this was over with she could sleep that soundly. After she grabbed her briefcase, she returned to the kitchen and sank into her chair.

"I'll start tonight, then work on this until I hear about the verdict. I should work on my next case, but I don't think I can do it justice with everything happening around me."

Cade took a swig of his coffee. "That's understandable."

The silence in the house urged her to utilize this time to see where she and Cade stood in their relationship. At the least they needed to decide what to do about Michelle. Now that her daughter knew, Tory felt she couldn't keep it a secret from others. She would have to tell Derek's parents. She understood why Derek didn't let Cade talk to her when he called. All that had occurred with her being pregnant that led to bed rest the last month and the fast wedding had put a strain on her, and her body reacted. She didn't want to pretend something that wasn't right, and she couldn't ask Michelle to.

As she signed in to her work network, she said, "When this is over, I'll be telling Derek's parents that you were Michelle's biological father. I'd wanted to tell them years ago, but Derek didn't want them to know. I respected his wishes."

Cade peered up from the laptop and stopped typing. "Derek always had a lot of pride."

"He couldn't have children. I think that embarrassed him, letting others know that he was infertile."

"That explains a lot. Derek once talked to me about having enough kids to make a basketball team."

"That many?"

"Yep. Of course, then I had to one-up him and tell him I wanted a football team. That changed when I came back from the war. I didn't have what it took to be a dad to even one child."

"Detective Alexander served later than you. I've heard him tell Paul he appreciated his marine training, especially since he was a military police officer, but he was glad he didn't have any children. He didn't like how the world was going."

"There was a time I felt that way, then as I grew in my faith, I'd wished I did have children and helped to raise someone who would make a difference."

His intense look captured her, and time seemed to come to a standstill. "You've got Michelle now," she whispered as her love for him swelled into her throat.

"Yeah, but where do I stand with her?"

"Your relationship might be better than mine at the moment." Tory twisted in her chair so she could face him. "When we're not dealing with some kind of mad man, we'll talk with Michelle."

Turning toward her, he took her hand in his. "Where do *we* stand?" His fingers delved into her hair, and he cupped her head. "I never really ever fell out of love with you. We've changed over the years, but that's to be expected. I love you even more now. I don't want any misunderstandings between us. I want you to know exactly how I feel about you. I want to spend the rest of my life with you." Leaning forward, he bridged the distance between them and kissed her as he pulled her closer. "I'm discovering I need to express how I feel rather than wait for a better time."

She laid her palm against his jawline, feeling the slight roughness of his day-old beard. "I love you. And I don't think I ever stopped loving you. I didn't understand what happened fifteen years ago to us, and let my anger and insecurity dictate what I should do. If I'd listened to my heart and not my head, I would have waited. I want us to be a family, but our daughter has a say in that. She's gone through so much turmoil recently."

"As hard as this is to say, I agree. If we have to wait until she leaves for college, then we will. I want you as my wife. No one else."

Happiness swept through her, chased by fear that Michelle would never accept Cade at least as her husband.

After catching a few hours of sleep midmorning, Cade rose from the kitchen table and stretched, his muscles protesting the inactivity. "I can't find where Officer Sims grew up. I know he was born in El Paso, but he and his family left there when he was eight. That's ten years unaccounted for."

"How about the others at the station?" Tory arched her back and rolled her shoulders. "Police work is tedious."

"Yes, it can be." Cade looked at his list of employees of the police department. "I'm down to the last two. I'm not going into as much depth for anyone who has been here all his life, which is surprisingly not as many as I thought."

"Remember how much El Rio has grown since we were teenagers."

"Have you found anything?" Cade sat again in front of the laptop.

"I keep going back to a copy of cases that have either the judge or Officer Sims involved. Each one involves the biker gang in some way. I'm part of some of them but not all. What if someone is trying to hurt the biker gang? Setting them up?"

"Because we haven't been able to make a conviction stick with a lot of them, especially Mederos and his lieutenants?"

Tory nodded. "I know I'm probably reaching, but

maybe we should think outside the box. Look at the only ones involved with Mederos. Everything seems to revolve around that man. What if the person can't get to Mederos but wants the man to pay for something. It's not like Mederos isn't responsible for a lot of bad things happening."

"Okay. I'd already looked at Roberts, and he's dead. Dead men don't kill. Lindsey has disappeared from El Rio months ago."

"But what about his family? Clarence Roberts's trial was different from the others I convicted in the gang. It was too easy. I remember the young man. He didn't have an alibi when the rape took place. Usually Mederos's gang members had alibis, often through lies and intimidation of others." Tory could remember his demeanor change through the short trial from cocky to apprehensive.

"What was the evidence?"

"The woman picked him out of a lineup, although I got the feeling she wasn't 100 percent sure, and an earring he often wore was found at the crime scene. He hardly said a word through the trial with a court appointed lawyer who botched the case. He should have challenged the woman's ID of Clarence as the rapist. At the time I was just glad to put a member of the gang in prison. But when I look at it from a different angle and take into consideration other cases with Mederos's minions, something was off."

"Who else?"

"Bobby Lindsey. You could never find him. What happened to him? He was one angry guy. I wasn't surprised he started working for Mederos. He was so angry and mean. Are you sure he isn't in El Rio?" She felt like she was grasping at straws. She was glad she didn't do investigating as a profession.

"If so, he has been hiding for six months. The last anyone saw him was at the beginning of summer. He isn't from around here, and I even checked Paris, Texas, where he grew up. I asked Blackwell and Jones about Lindsey too. Jones said he was there one day and gone the next."

"So he should stay on the list. We can't rule him out. Did you ever hear back about Matthew Thorne after he was picked up for a parole violation?"

Cade winced. "Yes. I forgot to tell you. So much has been going on. Thorne is a dead end. He has an alibi for Judge Parks's murder. He was three states away and picked up for drunk driving. He couldn't have done it."

"What about your list? Officer Sims lived in El Paso and so did Mederos at one time."

"But not the same time. I know that Mederos came to El Rio from Laredo and before that Van Horn."

"We could go ask Officer Sims. He's been at the station some. I saw him that day I came from the trial when Ben and Michelle were in Paul's office. He told me he couldn't sit around doing nothing while he recuperated. He hated being on medical leave."

Cade chuckled. "I know the feeling. When you're used to action and work, resting can be a jolt to your system. Not a bad idea. I'll finish up with the last three people at the station then if the verdict hasn't come in we should track down Officer Sims."

"Who else do you have?"

"Detective Alexander, Lieutenant Sanders and Officer McKay." Cade returned to his laptop.

Tory stood. "Kara's granddad should be here soon to

pick her up. Michelle will miss her, but hopefully this will end soon. I really think the threat to Michelle and me is over. It was connected to the trial. I'm going to let her go back to school next Monday." When Cade tensed, she added, "Unless you can convince me otherwise." Cade should have a say in Michelle's safety—her life.

"You're probably right. Unless the jury is still debating a verdict."

Tory started for the hallway. "Please don't say that. I'm starting to think Mederos got to one of the jurors although they have been sequestered since the trial began." As she made her way into the living room, her cell phone rang. It was Rachel. "Is the jury back?"

"Yes," her secretary said.

"I'll be right there." Tory backtracked to the kitchen. "Give me ten minutes to get ready, then I need to go to the courthouse, Cade."

He glanced up. "The verdict is in?"

"Yes."

Michelle came up behind Tory. "It is. I can't believe how excited I am to be going back to school. Can I tomorrow?"

"You should be able to by Monday but hold off celebrating until we hear the verdict and reassess the situation."

Michelle skirted Tory and went into the kitchen. "Cade, do you agree with that?"

Surprise flitted across his face. "Yes."

Michelle let out a loud sigh then went back into the living room.

"I hope she was asking not just because I'm guarding her but that I'm her father."

"Maybe it's a little of both." Tory left him sitting in

the kitchen, trying not to get too optimistic just yet. Maybe they would get their lives back soon.

Cade escorted Tory out of the courtroom after the guilty verdict had been declared. Mederos would be sentenced tomorrow. The press covering the trial immediately surrounded Tory.

A reporter stuck a microphone into Tory's face. "Does this mean the end of the recent violence?"

"I can't predict the future, but the right verdict was reached in this trial. A father who stood up against a person who terrorized others can sleep peacefully now."

Tory continued to answer a couple more questions as she walked with Cade toward the elevator. He blocked the reporters from trying to get on with them.

The second the doors swished closed, Tory collapsed back against the wall and shut her eyes. "That was the most intense few minutes waiting for the verdict. Justice has finally prevailed."

"Ready to celebrate?"

"Yes, but first I have something I need to do. Paul told me Officer Sims didn't come in today to help, so I thought we would stop by his house. Other than seeing him briefly the other day at the police station, I haven't had time to talk to him since he was shot."

Cade hesitated, not sure if she should until everything was wrapped up neatly.

"Cade, I need my life back. As I said before, I don't think I'm a target now. The trial is over. The star witness testified. Killing me won't change anything now. My death won't stop the harassment and fear the gang used to wield. Carlos Dietz was an example of what has to be done to stop crime. Paul told me another citizen has come forward to accuse Buck of shaking him down if he didn't pay his protection fee as expected. I think more store owners will come forward now."

"I haven't finished checking out Officer Sims."

"I'll be okay. You'll be with me. I can't see him harming me even if he was the station mole. What good would that do? Instead he would be covering his tracks. And besides, if he is the mole, why was he shot at? I was the target that day, not him. He took a bullet while guarding me. I'd like to stop at the bakery and bring him some chocolate fudge. I've heard he loves that."

"Fine. I know an argument I can't win." He tossed her a grin as they left the courthouse. "You're right," he continued after they were settled in the armored SUV. "Which means I'll have to return this and start looking for a car since the insurance company totaled mine."

"When we return to my house, are you and Ben leaving tonight?"

"Do you want me to?"

"Honestly, no. I don't want to stay at my place. Just walking by the bathroom gives me the chills."

"Then we'll stay at least for the night and have that talk with Michelle. You two can always come to my ranch until you figure out what you're going to do."

After picking up the fudge at the bakery, Tory remained silent on the drive to Officer Sims's house, her teeth worrying her lower lip.

At Sims's place he turned to her. "What's going on?"

"I have no idea how Michelle will feel about us."

"Neither do I, but don't worry. It won't change the outcome, but it might give you a few gray hairs."

She laughed. "Gray hairs. I hate to burst your bubble. But I found a couple last month."

He winked, said, "I won't tell anyone," then walked with her to the officer's small home, Sims's car in the driveway.

"You just wait until Michelle starts dating. Then you'll have your share of gray hairs."

This brief repartee reminded him of when they used to date. He would tease her, and she would tease him right back. Maybe this would work between them.

As Cade rang the bell, he clasped Tory's hand. The first time in a long while, he had something to really look forward to—reconnecting with Tory and getting acquainted with his daughter. Before El Rio, his life had consisted of work and then more work. Now he might have more.

"Maybe Officer Sims isn't home." Tory glanced back at his car in the driveway. "Maybe someone picked him up."

Cade knocked on the door, then went to the left while Tory stepped to the right to check through the window. No one in the kitchen.

"Cade!"

He rushed to Tory's side and saw Sims, lying on the living room floor, part of his body blocked by a chair, but not his chest covered in blood. "Call 911."

He tried to kick the door open, but it didn't budge, so he picked up a porch chair, said, "Stand back," and smashed it into the window. The glass shattered, and he quickly began knocking out what still remained until it was safe to climb inside as Tory finished calling the emergency in. "Stay in the SUV." When she didn't move, he added, "Whoever did this may still be inside."

Tory started for the SUV. Cade waited until she opened the front passenger door before he climbed through the gaping hole into the living room. The stench of blood flooded his nostrils. He moved toward Sims. Finally seeing a full view of the police officer, Cade knew Sims wasn't alive. Not only was there a wound in his chest, but also he'd been shot in the face.

Quickly he checked for a pulse to make sure he was dead, then he withdrew his gun to search the house. When he turned to check the living room, his gaze fell on the wall. The word *Traitor* was written in blood.

Tory stared at the window where Cade disappeared inside. Had someone finished the job of killing Officer Sims that had been started last week at the courthouse? Why did the person come after the police officer? He wasn't guarding her anymore. Would she be next? Cade? She punched the button to lock all the car doors.

A rustling sound directly behind Tory alerted her that she wasn't alone. She grabbed the handle and started to open the door.

"Don't do it."

Her mouth went dry at the same time her heartbeat accelerated. "Detective Alexander? What's…"

"Shut up. I have to finish this. My little brother died because of Mederos and his gang. I couldn't protect him when we were separated after our parents died, but I will avenge his murder. You both were too close to the truth. It was only a matter of time before you figured it all out."

"Figure out what?"

"That I killed the judge and framed Pedro. Mederos doesn't get to have his little brother. And once I found out Sims was the mole, I took care of him too."

Keep him talking. Maybe Cade would figure out

something was wrong. "Why did you think we were close?"

"After processing your house, I put a couple of listening devices in your place." Alexander waved his gun at her. "Call Morgan and have him come out to the car. Now!"

The savagery in the order emphasized if she did Cade would die.

Too.

She couldn't leave Michelle without a parent. "No. I won't."

A click echoed through her mind as she brought the handle down and readied herself to leap from the car.

A muffled shot, then a pain spread out from her chest. The world spun, and she slumped against the door.

Darkness rushed in. Her eyes closed.

TWELVE

Having worked his way through Sims's house, Cade noted expensive items—like a state-of-the-art big screen television and sound system—a cop couldn't afford on his salary. Was Sims the mole? Was that what traitor meant? Who murdered him? Why?

Cade headed for the living room to unlock the door for the police then to assess the crime scene until help arrived. They should be here any minute. Standing over the body, he examined the area around it. His gaze lit upon a toothpick several feet away.

When he lifted his eyes, Detective Alexander came through the entrance.

"You got here fast," Cade said, starting to relax.

A memory flashed across his mind of the detective chewing on a toothpick as Alexander raised his gun.

Cade dove behind the couch as a series of bullets exploded from Alexander's weapon, two ripping a hole through the sofa's back cushion. One missed him by inches.

Quickly Cade crawled to the end of the piece of furniture, anticipating the detective coming his way. He peered around the couch. The second he saw Alexander, Cade squeezed off a shot.

The detective stumbled and went down, raising his gun again.

Cade pulled the trigger a second time as flashing red lights announced help was here.

Tory!

He jumped to his feet, snatched Alexander's gun from the floor a few feet away from his still body and raced out of the house. Paul exited the first squad car. But Cade headed for the SUV. Tory was leaning against the door.

With each stride he took, his pulse rate increased. *Please, God. Don't take Tory away.*

Michelle flew through the hospital waiting room doors straight into Cade's arms. He hugged her, tears misting his eyes. This was not the way he wanted to reconnect with his daughter.

Uncle Ben followed her into the waiting room.

When Michelle leaned back and looked up at him, her eyes were red from crying—Cade's heart broke all over again. First when he held Tory, a faint pulse beating. Then a second time when the paramedics had to shock her heart. In the few seconds he waited to see her life signs recharge, he wanted to trade places with Tory.

"How is she?" Michelle's voice cracked on a sob. "No one would tell me anything."

"Let's sit down. I don't know much myself other than—" he settled on a two-seat couch "—she's in surgery. She lost a lot of blood, but the bullet didn't hit her heart."

All color washed from Michelle's face. "Who did this?"

"Tom Alexander, a police detective."

Michelle sucked in a sharp breath. "Why?"

"I'm not sure of the details, but the police chief is sticking close by Alexander waiting to see if he can talk to him."

Michelle buried her face against Cade's chest and cried.

Uncle Ben sat across from them. "Can I get you anything? Coffee?"

Numbly Cade shook his head. The only thing he wanted was Tory, and that wasn't something his uncle could give him. The pain in his chest spread as though he'd been shot, not Tory.

Cade leaned back against the wall opposite Tory's hospital room. The doctor was inside with Tory. Thankfully she had awakened from the surgery, but it wasn't going to be an easy recovery. Two inches and he would be mourning her loss. Still could.

Paul walked toward him, carrying two cups of coffee. "How are you holding up?"

"As well as to be expected."

"Where are Michelle and Ben?"

"Getting lunch. They're going to bring me back something to eat. What brings you here? Tory can't have visitors yet."

"I came here to give you an update on Sims and Alexander. I'm tying up the loose ends."

"I appreciate you following up on if Sims was the mole. Not only did Alexander kill Sims but Pedro Mederos. Match the DNA from the toothpicks found at both crime scenes. I'm sure it will be Alexander's."

"Working on it. We have enough evidence to lock him up on murder charges. The gun used to murder Sims was on Alexander and it matches the one that killed Judge Parks. So why did he kill Pedro and Sims?"

"And shot Tory? I have a theory that Tory and I were working on. Was Sims the mole?"

Frowning, Paul nodded. "We found cash under the floorboards as well as an offshore banking account in the Cayman Islands. He'd been handsomely paid for years by the Mederos gang."

"He was the one Blackwell was talking about, the one that Mederos had a past with."

"Yes. No wonder we had a hard time catching Mederos or his gang members. Sims was there letting him know what we were doing and thinking." Paul's voice toughened almost to a growl.

"So did you find the sniper gun Alexander used to shoot Sims and Tory at the courthouse?"

"Yes."

"There are a couple of cases you should look into— Clarence Roberts and Bobby Lindsey. They were both members of the gang and they went to jail. Roberts was killed in prison. The other has disappeared. He was working for Mederos, but no one in the gang knows where he is, at least they say that. See if Tomas and Leon know anything about what happened to Lindsey. Or anyone else who will talk in the gang. I suspect Lindsey didn't just disappear but was killed."

"What are you thinking?"

"Sims was a mole, but why did Alexander murder Judge Parks? Let's see if there are any connections among Alexander, Roberts or Lindsey. Is this some kind of revenge on Alexander's part?"

The ping of the elevator caught Cade's attention. As Michelle and Uncle Ben approached, Cade said, "Probably or why go after the judge. Dig into their backgrounds. I've got a feeling about this. Alexander had an agenda that he used the trial of Mederos to further. Have you been able to question Alexander yet?"

"No, but I will. The doctor will let me know when I can, and I'll be in his hospital room pronto. Has Tory said anything yet?"

"No, she's been too groggy or sleeping. I'll let you know if Alexander told her anything."

Paul glanced at the pair walking toward them. "I'll take care of the wrap-up. You have more important things to take care of. Don't mess it up this time."

"I'm not planning to."

Cade met Michelle and Uncle Ben at the door into Tory's room. "The doctor is with her."

At that moment her physician came out into the corridor.

"Is Mom all right?"

The older gentleman smiled. "She is doing much better. In fact, she was asking for you and Mr. Morgan."

Michelle grabbed Cade's hand and said, "Let's go in, Cade and Uncle Ben."

"I think you two should go in. I'll be back in an hour or so." Uncle Ben left.

Cade entered Tory's room with his daughter, side by side as though they were a family.

The sight of Tory in the hospital bed robbed him of a decent breath. When he found her in the car, he'd never been so afraid in his life. He couldn't lose her a second time. But the Lord answered his prayers.

"She's asleep again." Michelle plopped down on the small couch.

"She'll be doing a lot of that. Her body needs it to recover."

"She will get better, won't she? I know the doctor said she would be okay..." His daughter bit her bottom lip. "I can't lose her. What if she dies—I'll be alone."

"She isn't going to die. I'm here for you."

"Why didn't you want to be my father before?"

"Your mother didn't realize I had been on a secret mission in a war zone when she tried to let me know she was pregnant. She married Derek so you would have a father. Derek was a great dad for you. I couldn't disrupt that. I followed you from a distance. Remind me to show you my album I have of you growing up."

"Really?"

"Your dad and Uncle Ben sent me pictures of you as you grew up."

"So you cared?" Her eyes shone.

"I love you and have since you were born."

"Do you love Mom?"

"Yes, I always have. Are you okay with that?"

Michelle stared at Tory for a long moment then looked at him. "Yes. Dad would want her to be happy."

Cade hugged his daughter against him. *Thank You, God.*

Ten days later, Tory sat on her couch in her living room minus all the bugs discovered planted by Alexander. The scent of Caribbean chicken stew filled her house. Her stomach rumbled. She knew she was getting better because her appetite was returning. She hated being an invalid, being on the sidelines while everyone else wrapped up the biggest case of her career.

Ben had been staying with her and Michelle while Cade threw himself into the investigations that stemmed from Leon and Tomas turning state's evidence and Detective Alexander confessing his part in the events. He murdered Judge Parks because he was the judge on his young brother's trial—Bobby Lindsey. Alexander also killed Officer Sims because he was the informant for the biker gang. Mederos ordered Bobby's death last summer because he was talking to Alexander, feeding him information on the drug deliveries. Sims had ratted on him to the gang leader. Alexander wanted to bring the gang down and knew legally it would be almost impossible, so when Mederos was on trial he saw an opportunity to make certain people pay for what happened to Bobby. Everything else that happened to her and Michelle was because of the gang.

Just thinking about the past month made her head ache. She massaged her temple. The sound of the front door opening announced Cade was finally here for dinner.

He came into the living room, a gleam in his eyes. "At the rate we're going, you'll be one busy DA when you return to work." He took the place next to her, leaned toward her and kissed her. "Now that makes it all worth it."

"I know we're going to talk to Michelle tonight, but you and I need to first."

He pulled back, his smile gone. "You're having second thoughts about us?"

"No. I have to make a decision, and I need to talk to you about it. I'm thinking about resigning as the DA."

"You are? That'll make Michelle happy, but will you be okay with the decision?"

"I've worked as an assistant DA and DA for over ten years. I've been part of taking down the Mederos gang that has been plaguing our county. I've done my part to make this place safe. I need to take a break, at least until Michelle grows up and leaves home. She woke up last night with a nightmare. She won't sleep in her room anymore. She shares mine. I don't want her to live in fear."

"Okay. What's holding you back?" He relaxed and put his arm around her.

"What do I do with myself? I've worked most of my adult life."

He turned her head toward him. "You can work for Legal Aid and help people who can't afford a lawyer. Or, you can marry me and have another child."

She laughed. "How about both?"

"Whatever makes you happy." He pulled her against him and gave her a kiss that expressed all his love for her.

EPILOGUE

One year later

"Mom, Uncle Ben is taking me to the gym for the game." Michelle popped her head into Benjamin's room at the ranch. "You and Dad are coming to see me play, right?"

"I wouldn't miss it. I'm feeding your brother and will be ready when Cade comes home."

"Great. See you in a while."

The sound of a door slamming shut resonated through the house.

"Your big sister doesn't know how to softly close her door."

Benjamin had fallen asleep while nursing. Tory wiped his mouth and rose from the rocking chair. He could sleep through a lot of noise. She wouldn't be surprised if he did through the whole game. After putting her ten-week-old son in his carrier, she packed everything she'd need when they went out. Wipes. Diapers—

"I love watching you with him." Cade's voice interrupted her packing.

Tory smiled and let him sweep her into his embrace. "You're home a little early."

"I wanted to make sure I didn't miss the first game of the tournament. I can't get enough of watching Michelle play basketball. She's really good."

"And like any proud papa, you want to be there from the beginning cheering her on."

Cade snuggled her against him. "You know me so well. How was our son today?"

"Missing you like his mama." Tory brought his head down so she could kiss him. "I love you more each day."

"And I love you." Cade kissed her. "You don't miss being DA, do you?"

"You, Michelle and Benjamin are all I need, but my part-time work with Legal Aid has been great." She gave him a peck on his cheek. "Let's go or we'll never hear the end of it from Michelle for being late."

* * * * *

If you loved this exciting romantic suspense,
pick up these other stories
from Margaret Daley's previous miniseries
ALASKAN SEARCH AND RESCUE

THE YULETIDE RESCUE
TO SAVE HER CHILD
THE PROTECTOR'S MISSION
STANDOFF AT CHRISTMAS

Available now from Love Inspired Suspense!

Find more great reads at www.LoveInspired.com.

Dear Readers,

High-Risk Reunion is the first book in my series, Lone Star Justice, about the Texas Rangers who are part of the state police in Texas. I had the privilege of visiting the Texas Rangers' office in Garland, where I interviewed a Ranger about the job. There are 150 commissioned Texas Rangers for the whole state of Texas. They investigate murder, fraud, robbery, corruption of a public official and other crimes, as well as protect the governor of Texas and state and federal officials.

High-Risk Reunion is about what can happen when you keep a secret. Tory had to deal with the secret of Michelle's birth. She made some difficult decisions when she was young and years later her daughter learned of the truth. When Michelle found out who her real father was, it led to her doing something foolish. The truth may be hard to tell, but in the long run it is better to do it. Secrets have a way of coming out.

I love hearing from readers. You can contact me at margaretdaley@gmail.com or at P. O. Box 2074, Tulsa, OK 74101. You can also learn more about my books at http://www.margaretdaley.com. I have a newsletter that you can sign up for on my website.

Best wishes,
Margaret

REQUEST YOUR FREE BOOKS!
2 FREE RIVETING INSPIRATIONAL NOVELS
PLUS 2 FREE MYSTERY GIFTS

Love Inspired
SUSPENSE
RIVETING INSPIRATIONAL ROMANCE

YES! Please send me 2 FREE Love Inspired® Suspense novels and my 2 FREE mystery gifts (gifts are worth about $10). After receiving them, if I don't wish to receive any more books, I can return the shipping statement marked "cancel." If I don't cancel, I will receive 4 brand-new novels every month and be billed just $4.99 per book in the U.S. or $5.49 per book in Canada. That's a savings of at least 17% off the cover price. It's quite a bargain! Shipping and handling is just 50¢ per book in the U.S. and 75¢ per book in Canada.* I understand that accepting the 2 free books and gifts places me under no obligation to buy anything. I can always return a shipment and cancel at any time. Even if I never buy another book, the two free books and gifts are mine to keep forever.

123/323 IDN GH5Z

Name	(PLEASE PRINT)
Address	Apt. #
City	State/Prov.	Zip/Postal Code

Signature (if under 18, a parent or guardian must sign)

Mail to the **Reader Service:**
IN U.S.A.: P.O. Box 1867, Buffalo, NY 14240-1867
IN CANADA: P.O. Box 609, Fort Erie, Ontario L2A 5X3

**Are you a current subscriber to Love Inspired® Suspense books
and want to receive the larger-print edition?
Call 1-800-873-8635 or visit www.ReaderService.com.**

* Terms and prices subject to change without notice. Prices do not include applicable taxes. Sales tax applicable in N.Y. Canadian residents will be charged applicable taxes. Offer not valid in Quebec. This offer is limited to one order per household. Not valid for current subscribers to Love Inspired Suspense books. All orders subject to credit approval. Credit or debit balances in a customer's account(s) may be offset by any other outstanding balance owed by or to the customer. Please allow 4 to 6 weeks for delivery. Offer available while quantities last.

Your Privacy—The Reader Service is committed to protecting your privacy. Our Privacy Policy is available online at www.ReaderService.com or upon request from the Reader Service.
We make a portion of our mailing list available to reputable third parties that offer products we believe may interest you. If you prefer that we not exchange your name with third parties, or if you wish to clarify or modify your communication preferences, please visit us at www.ReaderService.com/consumerchoice or write to us at Reader Service Preference Service, P.O. Box 9062, Buffalo, NY 14240-9062. Include your complete name and address.

LIS15

*When former navy nurse Stella Silverstone returns to
her hometown to care for her grandmother, someone
wants her out of the way—preferably dead.
But Chance Miller, owner of the security and rescue
agency where she works, will put his own life on the
line to guard her.*

*Read on for a sneak preview of
THE CHRISTMAS TARGET by Shirlee McCoy,
available November 2016 from Love Inspired Suspense!*

"I need to keep Beatrice safe," Stella murmured, trying to
refocus her thoughts, keep them where they needed to be.
"The guy who attacked me is still out there, and I can't
count on him not returning."

Chance heard the worry in Stella's voice, and the
weariness. She wasn't asking for help, but they both
knew she needed it.

"We'll keep her safe."

We'll keep you safe, too was on the tip of his tongue,
but he didn't say it. Stella prided herself on being able to
handle just about anything. She didn't like needing help,
but she'd take it when necessary. This was one of the few
times when it absolutely was.

"I appreciate that, Chance, but Cooper and his
department—"

"Aren't going to be able to provide twenty-four-hour
protection. HEART can."

"At what cost? Another job? A client who really needs your help not getting it because you're here helping me?"

"We have plenty of manpower, Stella, and you know it. If you don't want us here, you'll have to come up with a better reason than that." She wouldn't. Because she knew HEART could do what needed to be done faster and better than just about anyone else.

She shrugged.

"If you want HEART out, say so," he prodded, and she sighed.

"I would, but I do need the help. Much as I hate to admit it, my brain isn't functioning at a fast enough pace to keep my grandmother safe."

Whomever the attacker was, he had motive, he had means and he wasn't messing around. Two attempts in a few hours meant he was also desperate.

For what?

That was the question Chance needed to answer.

If he did, he'd have the answer to everything else.

Except what he was going to do once Stella was safe and there was nothing standing between them but her reluctance to be hurt and his decision to let her walk away.

Don't miss
THE CHRISTMAS TARGET by Shirlee McCoy,
available November 2016 wherever
Love Inspired® Suspense books and ebooks are sold.

www.LoveInspired.com

LISEXP1016

SPECIAL EXCERPT FROM

Love Inspired

What happens when a Texas Ranger determined to stay single meets a pregnant widow who unwittingly works her way into his heart?

Read on for a sneak preview of the second book in the
LONE STAR COWBOY LEAGUE: BOYS RANCH
miniseries, **THE RANGER'S TEXAS PROPOSAL**
by **Jessica Keller**.

"What can I do for you, Officer?" Josie Markham's tone said she didn't really want to do anything for him. Ever.

He raised his eyebrows.

"White hat. Boots. White starched shirt. And that belt's the type they only issue to Texas Rangers." She gestured toward his holster. "I hope you weren't trying to be undercover."

"Good eye." He extended his hand. She narrowed her gaze but shook it. "Heath Grayson. I'm a friend of Flint's."

In the space of a heartbeat, her hesitant expression vanished and was replaced by wide-eyed concern. "Did something else happen at the boys ranch?" She shifted from around the wheelbarrow. "What are we waiting for? If something's wrong, let's go."

Once she moved away from the wheelbarrow, he saw her stomach. Pregnant. Very pregnant. Flint had mentioned Josie was widowed, but he'd left out the little detail that she was with child. So a recent widow.

LIEXPI016

Had she been in the barn alone…doing chores?

"Let me help you with your chores," Heath said.

Josie's jaw dropped. "What about the boys ranch?"

"The ranch is fine."

"Why didn't you say so? You about gave me a heart attack." She laid her hand on her chest and took a few deep breaths. Then her eyes skirted back up to capture his. "If the ranch is fine, why exactly are you here then?"

She fanned her face and dragged in huge amounts of oxygen through her mouth as if she was having a hard time getting it into her lungs.

Now he'd done it. Gone and gotten a pregnant woman all worked up. Did he need to find her a chair? A drink of water? Rush her to the hospital? What a terrible feeling, being out of control. It was disconcerting.

"Are you all right, ma'am? What do you need?"

"I'm fine. Just fine." She laughed. "You should see your face, though." She pointed up at him and covered her mouth, hiding her wide grin. Her warm brown eyes shone with mischief. "Now you look like you're the one having a heart attack. Relax there, Officer. It was only a figure of speech." Her laugh was a high sound, full of joy. Josie laughed with her whole self, without holding anything back.

Heath wanted to hear it again.

Don't miss
THE RANGER'S TEXAS PROPOSAL
by Jessica Keller, available November 2016 wherever
Love Inspired® books and ebooks are sold.

www.LoveInspired.com